DEVIL'S RANGE

Caleb Ross had agreed to join his old friend Tom Watson as a ranching partner in Ghost Creek, and arrives full of optimism. But he rides into big trouble. Tom has been gunned down by Jack Sweeney of the Rawl range, mentor in mayhem to Scott Rawl . . . Enraged, Caleb heads for the ranch seeking vengeance for Tom's murder. But, up against a crooked law force and formidable opposition, he'll have to be quick and clever if he's to survive . . .

SKEETER DODDS

DEVIL'S RANGE

Complete and Unabridged

LINFORD
Leicester

First published in Great Britain in 2006 by
Robert Hale Limited
London

First Linford Edition
published 2007
by arrangement with
Robert Hale Limited
London

British Library CIP Data

Dodds, Skeeter
    Devil's Range.—Large print ed.—
    Linford western library
    1. Western stories
    2. Large type books
    I. Title
    823.9'2 [F]

    ISBN 978–1–84617–699–9

Published by
F. A. Thorpe (Publishing)
Anstey, Leicestershire

Set by Words & Graphics Ltd.
Anstey, Leicestershire
Printed and bound in Great Britain by
T. J. International Ltd., Padstow, Cornwall

This book is printed on acid-free paper

1

'That's Rawl water you're filling your canteen with, mister!'

Caleb Ross ignored the man's gruff rebuke and continued filling his canteen.

'You deaf?' the man growled.

'No,' Ross replied quietly. 'I just don't listen to fellas who are ill-mannered.'

'That a fact!'

'Surely is, friend.'

'I ain't your friend, and you're about to find that out, mister.'

Ross heard the jingle of spurs as the man dismounted. He straightened up and turned slowly to face his mean-eyed challenger, a brash young buck who had all the cockiness of a man who had inherited rather than earned his swagger.

'Don't want no touble,' Ross said. He

strolled to his horse and tied the canteen to his saddle horn. 'I'll be on my way.'

'Not with Rawl water, you won't,' the man grated.

Two other men came from the cover of trees on the creek's slope.

'What d'ya think we should do with this interloper, Jack?'

The snake-eyed man whom he had addressed rode forward.

'Well, Scott, we could string him up, I guess. He ain't no horse-thief. But stealing water in cow country in the middle of a dry spell sure ranks with horse-thieving, I reckon.

'Or . . .'

'Yeah, Jack,' the man called Scott sniggeringly encouraged.

' . . . we could brand him.'

'Just like a cow,' the second man of the duo who had ridden out of the trees suggested. 'Like that fella we caught crossing the south pasture a coupla days ago.'

'That sure was fun.' Jack chuckled.

'Yeah,' the second of the duo said. 'Smelled worse than a darn cow when that branding iron burned him.'

The man called Scott (at a guess his second name was Rawl, Ross reckoned) laughed meanly. 'That was because he shit himself, Barney.'

He pinched his nostrils.

'Wheeew! That was sure some stink.'

'Worse than a herd of longhorns cutting loose together,' Jack said, rocking in his saddle.

'Sure was,' Scott agreed.

'Hurts real bad,' Barney said. 'A hot brandin' iron. But not as much as the bullet Jack put in his gut.'

'Whoa, now,' Scott growled, grabbing the reins of Caleb Ross's mare. 'You ain't going nowhere until you pour that Rawl water back in the creek, mister.'

'Water is God's gift,' Caleb Ross said quietly.

'Yeah,' his impeder snarled. 'Well, the way I see it is, that God's name ain't Rawl, so that don't give him any right to give away Rawl water.'

He slapped his knee and guffawed.

'Tell ya what, stranger. When you meet him, which, if you don't pour that water back in the creek is going to be pretty soon, you can tell him that Rawl water ain't for giving away to every nogood trespassing on Rawl range.'

Scott Rawl glanced to the men riding with him, flanking Caleb Ross. Scott Rawl himself cut off his retreat from the creek.

'I'm waiting,' Rawl growled.

'The water stays in the canteen, fella,' Caleb Ross said, in the quiet way he spoke when his patience was running out.

Scott Rawl, obviously not used to defiance, was taken aback, as were the men with him; men who now awaited with interest the outcome of the stranger's dogged non-compliance with Rawl's demand. When he overcame his surprise at Ross's intransigence, Rawl's manner was a hundred times meaner.

'Are you prepared to die for a canteen of water?' he put to Ross.

'The water doesn't count,' Ross said. 'But a man's refusal to be pushed around does.'

The Rawl riders' surprise turned to outright dismay, and all eyes fixed on Scott Rawl. Caleb Ross had, perhaps unwisely, seeing that the odds of surviving any outbreak of hostilities were stacked mountain high against him, backed Rawl into a corner, and that was a dangerous place to back any coward into. Right now his entire future as these men's unquestioned leader was at stake. Rawl's pride had already been dented by his resistence, and that left him with only two options. He could back down and hang his head low and leave with his tail between his legs. Or he could maintain his challenge and risk dying.

'I'll probably only get one shot off, mister. But that single bullet will end up in your heart, if you push this any further,' Ross said.

Scott Rawl's cockiness was jolted, and his sun-burnished face developed a shade of grey under the bronze. He was a bully and a coward, who had lived under the illusion that he had the kind of grit that he was now finding out he didn't have. Backed up right into the last inch of room in the corner into which Caleb Ross had forced him, Scott Rawl became an even more dangerous man than he had been a few seconds before.

His reaction was the expected one.

'That's still Rawl water in your canteen, mister. And if it's not back in the creek on the count of three,' he spread his legs and let his gunhand drop, 'I'm going to kill you, you smart-mouthed bastard!'

Caleb Ross's consideration of Scott Rawl was unflinching.

'Then I guess you can verify with God first hand that the water in that creek is everyman's right,' Ross said. 'Because you're going to meet him before I do.'

Ross's flinty response caused pure astonishment.

'You must want to die real bad, fella,' said the man Rawl had addressed as Jack.

'You gotta a hole in your head,' Barney added. 'There's three guns agin your one.'

Caleb Ross shrugged. 'Well, it only takes a second to pull a trigger, gents. I'll be happy if your boss goes with me.' He fixed a steely stare on Scott Rawl. 'And I'll make damn sure he does.'

A greasy sweat was added to Scott Rawl's grey pallor. Tension as sharp as the point of a needle crackled in the creek as the breathless stand-off dragged on.

'You ain't goin' to take this hobo's lip, are ya, Scott?' Barney wanted to know.

Rawl shot a snake-poison glance at the man who had had the impudence to ask the question he did not want asked.

'What's the problem, Scott?'

The woman's voice broke the impasse, which was just about on its last gasp and about to erupt in gunfire.

The woman was older than Scott Rawl, but there was no mistaking their sibling relationship. She skilfully negotiated the steep shale track down from the highest point of the creek.

'Stay outta this, Sis,' Scott Rawl ordered the woman when she reached the creek proper. His laughter was disparaging. 'Don't you have a pie to bake? Or a carpet to dust?'

The woman introduced herself to Caleb Ross.

'Sarah Rawl. Who would you be?'

Ross respectfully touched the brim of his hat. 'The name's Caleb Ross, ma'am.'

'You're trespassing on Rawl range,' she said sternly. 'Did you know that?'

'The cows didn't tell me.' Ross snorted.

'A smart mouth won't help you any,' Sarah Rawl said.

'Caught him stealing Rawl water, Sarah,' Scott Rawl put in.

'If you've got a reasonable explanation, I'll listen,' Sarah Rawl told Caleb Ross.

'For trespassing? Or stealing water, ma'am?'

Sarah Rawl's features hardened. 'Both!'

'Where I come from, ma'am,' Ross said. 'Folk are hospitable to a travelling stranger. They don't begrudge a man slaking his thirst. A beast neither.'

'That's not an explanation,' Sarah Rawl said starchily. 'You saw Rawl boundaries and warning signs, didn't you?'

Caleb Ross nodded.

'Then why — ?'

'Simple,' Ross interjected. 'To go round Rawl range would add a day to my journey, which I figured was a day too long, ma'am. Especially when I had no ill-intent towards Rawl interests.'

'Ain't that enough for you, Sis?' Scott Rawl bawled. 'Him admitting brazenly that he knowingly trespassed.'

Sarah Rawl tossed back her mane of coal-black hair, her blue eyes, full of interest, fixed on the tall, dark-haired stranger, whose grey eyes were enlivened by a keen intelligence.

'It seems that my brother's got right on his side, Mr Ross,' she said. 'And you haven't given me any good reason to defend your trespass, or,' she glanced to the shallow creek, 'your theft,' she ended resolutely.

'I guess I haven't at that, m'am,' Caleb Ross conceded. 'But as I was saying to your brother before you intervened. I figure that water is part of God's creation, and therefore free for the taking.'

'We've had enough dancing around, mister,' Scott Rawl growled. 'Now get out of the way, Sarah. I'll deal with this tinhorn.'

'You move an inch either side of where you are right now,' Ross quietly warned Sarah Rawl, 'and you'll sign your brother's death warrant, ma'am.'

Sarah Rawl smiled, what Caleb Ross would call a heart-breaker smile.

'I'd say you're a mite out-numbered, Mr Ross,' she said pleasantly, secretly admiring Caleb Ross's grit, foolish though she reckoned it was. 'You must have a real hankering to thank the Lord personally for all that free water you've been purloining.'

'Well, ma'am,' Caleb Ross leaned on his saddle horn, 'you see, I've got a choice that ain't really a choice at all. I can ride out of this creek sucking air but dead inside because I'd be leaving my pride behind me. Or I can draw and not leave at all. But I'd have company, though it wouldn't be the company I'd have chosen. Because if I stay put, so does your hole-in-the-head brother.'

He held Sarah Rawl's gaze.

'I'll make damn sure of that, ma'am,' he promised.

'Why you — '

Sarah Rawl raised her hand to quieten Scott Rawl.

Caleb Ross leaned closer to Sarah Rawl.

'As I've been telling your brother, Miss Rawl. I reckon I'll only have time to get off one shot.' Caleb Ross's grey eyes became flinty specks of cold hardness. 'But I'll make damn sure that that single bullet will shatter your sibling's heart.'

He grinned.

'Ma'am.'

Sarah Rawl could not suppress the cold shiver that ran along her spine, and then passed deep inside her. She was left with no doubt at all that Caleb Ross would do as he said he would, if he was pushed too far. And she reckoned that he was close to his limit of tolerance now. So convinced was she that, instead of moving aside as Scott Rawl had demanded of her, she moved closer to Ross and restricted further her brother's line of fire.

'What the hell d'ya think you're playing at, Sis?' Scott Rawl demanded to know.

'We've got lots of water, Scott,' she said.

'Not enough, until the last drop from that bastard's canteen is back in the creek.' Scott Rawl snarled.

Caleb Ross shook his head.

'Your brother's got a real hankering to play a harp, ma'am.'

'Ride,' she said.

'The hell he will!' Rawl growled, enraged.

'Pa won't welcome trouble right now, Scott,' she reminded her brother.

'Pa is off in Washington trying to woo those senators into nominating him to run for political office.'

'That's why he won't like trouble right now, Scott,' she said.

Scott Rawl scoffed. 'It's no secret that Pa's lost his grit for cows, and wants to dress in fancy duds and cavort around Washington. He ain't ever going to ride Rawl range again, Sis.'

'Ma'am, I'll be leaving now,' Caleb Ross said. 'You'll be needing the creek to wash all that dirty linen and rattle all those skeletons I reckon are in the Rawl closet.'

'Some day that lippy style of yours will get you shot or strung up, Mr Ross,' Sarah Rawl opined spikily.

'You're probably right at that,' Caleb Ross concurred. 'Be seeing all you fine folk around.'

'Around?' Sarah Rawl asked pointedly. 'You're staying round here?'

'For a spell.'

'What's a spell?' she questioned Ross brusquely.

Ross shrugged. 'A spell.'

'That spell could become permanent,' Scott Rawl grated.

Caleb Ross fixed Scott Rawl with a lazy gaze.

'You know, ma'am,' he intoned. 'That brother of yours has godawful manners. Real pushy, too.'

'My advice,' Sarah Rawl said, 'is that you shorten your stay in these parts to the time it takes your horse to make it across the hills and out of Rawl sight, Mr Ross.'

'Must be catching,' Ross said, shaking his head. 'Bad manners.'

'You ain't going to insult a Rawl and get away with it,' Scott Rawl ranted, striding towards Ross. He grabbed the bullwhip looped round his saddle horn and unfurled it with a vicious snap. 'I'm going to take the skin off your back,' he promised Caleb Ross.

Ross's boot shot out and landed on Scott Rawl's chest. He pushed hard and sent Rawl tumbling backwards. The tension in the creek crackled. Pride dented, sullen and fresh out of good sense, Scott Rawl dived for his sixgun.

Caleb Ross's pistol might as well have been in his hand all the time, that was how fast it cleared leather. Scott Rawl froze and looked death in the face.

'Please, Mr Ross,' Sarah pleaded. 'He's just a hothead.'

It took a long moment of consideration before Caleb Ross slid the Colt .45 back in its holster.

'Thank you,' Sarah Rawl said.

'Don't crowd me again, son,' he told Scott Rawl. Caleb Ross tipped his hat, swung his horse and rode across the creek.

'Look out!'

Caleb Ross threw himself from the saddle on hearing Sarah Rawl's warning. He twisted in midair as he dropped to the creek. A bullet whined above him only inches from his head. His .45 blasted, and his would-be assassin, who had been hiding in the trees to back up Rawl's play, was hurled off his horse, most of his face and head gone.

Ross regained his horse.

'Obliged, ma'am,' he said.

Caleb Ross rode away.

'Never knowed a faster draw,' Barney said in awe. 'Jeez, we were proddin' death just now. I figure he'd have taken the three of us.'

'Shuddup,' Scott Rawl barked. 'I figure I could have taken him in a straight draw.'

'Sure you could, Mr Rawl,' Barney said, placatingly.

Jack Sweeney said nothing, but he was ready to concede that Barney Collins might be right. If there was a faster gun than Caleb Ross's, it might be his own.

Sarah Rawl was just thankful that she had been in time to intervene and save her hot-headed fool of a brother.

'Interesting times ahead, I'd say.' Jack Sweeney chuckled.

2

On reflection, as he rode away, Caleb Ross reckoned that he had made the kind of powerful enemies a man could do without, particularly a man as new to the territory as a newly minted cent. Scott Rawl's aggresssion had left him with little choice, but had he been wiser he could have used the arrival of Sarah Rawl on the scene as a chance to back off, using the presence of a lady as the reason to end the dispute. It would have been a credible and better alternative to now having Scott Rawl and his cohorts gunning for him. But maybe he wouldn't have to worry, if the shocked looks at how fast he'd drawn were anything to go by. However, inevitably in his experience, there would always be someone foolish or willing enough to challenge a man with a fast gun. It was not the start he needed or wanted.

There's grass round here that's greener and richer than any I've ever seen, Caleb. Ross took from his vest pocket the letter he had received three months previously, it having followed him around for almost twelve months before finding him. *Starting a ranch here would be real easy,* Tom Watson had enthused.

The letter went on to invite Ross to join him as his partner in setting up the ranch Tom had always dreamed of starting, bending his ear on a hundred cattle-drives about the fine cows he'd one day drive for himself.

Then he'd say:

'You and me together, Caleb. What'll we call the ranch?'

Each of them would suggest names that the other would argue about. And on like that it would go until they both fell asleep under the stars, Tom Watson still mumbling in his sleep about cows and grass and sparkling clear water.

Cresting a hill, Caleb Ross drew rein to look across a valley that seemed to spread into eternity. The scent of its fresh, lush grass filled his nostrils. And the creek where he had filled his canteen surely was sweet water.

He grinned.

'Looks like you've really found El Dorado, Tom.' he murmured. 'And I'm one hell of a lucky honcho that you've invited me to join you.'

He stuffed Watson's letter back in his vest pocket and rode on, eager now to renew his acquaintance with his old trail partner.

'Hold up, Mr Ross!'

On hearing Sarah Rawl's summons, Caleb drew rein. As he watched her negotiate the twisting canyon trail he was on, he was full of admiration for her skill with a horse. Many a man of his acquaintance would boast himself hoarse if he had a tenth of Sarah Rawl's know-how. As with packing a gun, some folk had a natural affinity with horses, and it was obvious that Sarah Rawl and horseflesh complemented each other.

'I thought our business was finished,

ma'am,' Ross said when she drew rein.

'You know anything about cows, Mr Ross?'

'I've driven the critters over most trails,' he said.

'Want a job working for the Rawl ranch?'

Caleb Ross was truly surprised by her offer of work.

'Didn't figure I'd be welcome,' he said.

'You leave Scott to me. I'll talk him round. The fact is I need a hard-as-nails foreman. And I figure that you just might be the man I'm looking for.'

Ross shook his head.

'For a good man Rawl pays top dollar, Mr Ross. Maybe even a little more,' she tempted.

'It ain't a question of money, Miss Rawl.'

'If it's Scott you're worried about — '

'It ain't Scott I'm worried about neither. Some day, if he's guided by his sister, I figure there'll be a good man come out of a cock-of-the-walk boy.'

21

'So what is it, Mr Ross? Why don't you want to ride for the Rawl brand? Most men round here would jump at the chance.'

'I might too, Miss Rawl,' Ross drawled. 'If I didn't have plans to start my own brand.'

Sarah Rawl was stunned.

'Your own brand?' She shook her head vehemently. 'That's a silly notion which you should ditch pretty quick, I reckon.'

'That so? Why would that be, ma'am?'

'Every blade of grass is Rawl grass round here. And without grass, it's pretty nigh impossible to fatten stock. And,' she said determinedly, 'Rawl isn't giving any grass away.'

'Do you know a place called Ghost Creek round here, Miss Rawl?'

Sarah Rawl's eyes flashed interest.

'Free land, I believe. Well, that's where my partner and me intend to raise the best cows in the territory.'

'Would this partner's name be

Watson?' Sarah Rawl enquired quietly. 'Tom Watson?'

'That's him. Tom Watson. Forgotten more about cows that most men ever knew.' His eyes held Sarah Rawl's. 'Now, if you were looking for a ramrod, how come you didn't offer the job to Tom long ago?'

'I've delayed you long enough, Mr Ross,' Sarah Rawl said brusquely. She swung her horse and galloped back along the trail in the direction from which she had come.

'Well now, what in tarnation do you make of that, Belle?' Ross asked his horse. The mare, used to Ross's mutterings on their long trails together, neighed. 'Yeah, I agree. Pretty strange behaviour, sure enough.'

His puzzlement over Sarah Rawl's swift and indeed stiff-backed departure was short-lived. He didn't know what corn he'd stepped on, and he did not much care. His mind returned, as it had a million times and always with greater pleasure than previously, to the upcoming meeting with Tom Watson and the venture he was about to become involved in with his old friend and trail partner. His one and only worry as he covered the miles to Ghost Creek (which he hoped he'd be able to find with the aid of the roughly drawn map Tom had included with his letter of invitation to join him) was that, owing to the delay in his letter's finding him, Tom Watson, figuring that his interest in ranching had waned, would have taken on a new partner. He had written back to Tom but had not got a reply. However, that was nothing unusual in a country where stagecoaches and trains, being the modes of conveyance for mail, were subject to continuous threat from outlaws. The mail was often rich in pickings. So posting a letter was a pretty hit-and-miss affair. A fella could only hope that his missive would reach its destination, rather than nurture any sense of certainty that it would. And, of course, from Tom Watson's point of view, he'd be thinking that his letter might never have reached Caleb.

Caleb Ross had another of the anxious spells that had haunted him in his long journey. The chance to partner Tom Watson had been a heaven-sent redemption from the drifting ways he had taken to in the last couple of years, making ends meet by doing menial chores and scooping the odd poker-pot, finding that more and more doors were closed against him, and that in more and more towns the law was ready to run him out as a saddle tramp.

His mind went back five years to when, on a trip with Tom to Dodge City, he had met Bridie Walsh, literally bumped into her, in fact. Having left the saloon with Tom, after taking on board more liquor than he could handle, he collided with Bridie as she emerged from the general store. He recalled her initial contempt for this drunk she was tussling with before they both fell on to the street. But through the rotgut haze, he knew that he was in the arms of the woman he would make his wife.

'Ain't goin' to happen, Caleb,' Tom Watson warned him two days later when, at the end of their trip to Dodge, he was heading off to hire out again on yet another cattle-drive. 'That woman would rather kiss a rattler than you.'

There was clear and unequivocal evidence to back up Tom's point of view. Because on the several occasions since he had bumped into Bridie, she had steadfastly rebuffed his attempts to befriend her.

'Never figured I'd see you moonin' and lovesick like you are now,' Watson had declared, a touch critically. 'Always figured that the only female you'd ever get close to was a darn cow.' He grinned. ''Ceptin' of course, a saloon woman, purely for relief.

'You take my advice, you'll saddle up and ride with me, Caleb,' he said sincerely, and added sagely: 'Broken hearts are darn hard to mend.'

Ross had known that Tom Watson

was probably right in what he said, and his advice to ride with him made good sense. However, good sense and lovesickness are not compatible bedfellows, and an aching heart has to be broken or gladdened, before it can start to beat again in a normal fashion.

'If you see sense,' Tom Watson said hopelessly, as Ross's attention was given over completely to Bridie Walsh's appearance from the dress-shop, 'we'll meet up in six weeks at Baker Flats, partner.'

'Baker Flats, Tom,' Ross said absently, as he hurried away to cut across Bridie's path on the boardwalk.

Tom Watson had ridden away, shaking his head.

'Never thought I'd see the day,' he muttered.

Determined not to be fobbed off this time, Caleb Ross stood in front of Bridie Walsh and blocked her path. When she shifted left, he shifted right. Right and he went left. And when

Bridie grasped the opportunity presented by the sheriff's emergence from his office and niftily rounded Ross, he danced ahead of her to block her path again.

'You're darn well going to hear what I have to say, Bridie,' he'd declared. 'So you might as well stand still while I say it. Otherwise we'll both get dizzy.'

'From what I've seen,' Bridie Walsh said, 'dizziness to you, Mr Ross, is quite a normal condition.'

'Haven't touched a drop in two days.'

'Empty pockets, no doubt,' she had flung back.

Caleb Ross immediately produced twenty dollars as proof of his intentional sobriety. 'And I'll not touch a drop again if you want, Bridie.'

'Is this hobo bothering you, Bridie?' the large-bellied sheriff asked, closing threateningly on Ross.

Caleb's eyes met Bridie's, and his heart sang out when the clear intention in them to seek the lawman's assitance melted.

'No, Andy,' she said. 'Mr Ross is no bother at all.'

'Sure?' the sheriff checked, his dislike of Ross evident.

'Certain, Andy,' Bridie had replied, in her soft Galway accent.

Ross remembered how he had stepped aside and Bridie had joined him, and how he had strutted along the boardwalk like a preening peacock with Bridie Walsh at his side, the envy of every man in Dodge City.

'Persistent devil, aren't you,' she murmured, a mischievous smile on her lips, and an impishness in her green eyes.

'That's what love does to a man,' he'd said.

'Love, indeed,' Bridie scoffed. 'Now you've got more blarney than I have.'

'It's true,' Ross assured her. 'Ever since I set eyes on you coming out of the general store.'

'Love! Is that what you'd call that drunken dance?'

'Marry me, Bridie!'

'Mar . . . You've taken leave of your senses.'

'You could have had me thrown in jail just now, but you didn't.'

'Pure and simple charity, that was,' she said cockily.

'And you troubled yourself to find out my name, Bridie. Like I did yours.'

There was a flash of colour in Bridie Walsh's cheeks that had pleased him no end.

'Don't get notions,' she said off-handedly. 'I got your name because I was thinking about asking the sheriff to charge you with drunken assault.'

'Lies!'

Bridie did not deny his charge.

'There's a travelling preacher in town,' Caleb Ross had said.

'A preacher,' Bridie exclaimed. 'I'm a good Irish Catholic. Any knot that needs tying has to be tied by a priest, and not a preacher.'

'If you agree to marry me, I'll find a priest, Bridie,' he said.

'And where, might I ask, would you

find a good man of the cloth in this den of inquity?'

'There's a mission about three days' ride from here. I'll saddle up right this minute, and be back in a week with a priest.'

'Ah, don't bother me, man,' Bridie chanted. 'It's all the stale whiskey in your gut that's confusing your brain! Be off now with yourself.'

'If you don't agree to marry me right now,' Caleb had declared. 'I'll hang around like your shadow for every second of every day until you do.'

'Have you nothing better to do?'

'Not until you marry me, Bridie Walsh.'

Bridie had laughed heartily. 'God forbid then that I'd waste your time, Mr Ross. I'll marry you. But you understand that when a Catholic marries, it's for better or for worse until the lid goes on the coffin. Is that understood?'

'I'll never want to leave your side, Bridie,' he'd promised.

'Try and I'll kill you, Caleb Ross! I'll

31

not be a fancy for a time, understand. No liquor except on special occasions. No cards. And no cavorting in saloons. I've noticed, in me short time in the American West, that in general men have the morals of the English aristocracy. A wife is for sons. But pleasure is got elsewhere.

'If you behave in that fashion, Caleb Ross, I'll make it so that you'll fit your saddle a lot more snugly than I reckon you do now. Is that understood?'

Caleb Ross smiled fondly now, as Bridie Walsh's words echoed back over time.

'Yes, ma'am,' he had readily agreed, knowing that any other woman would pale into insignificance alongside Bridie Walsh, and temptation would not be a problem that would bother him.

'Well, then,' she said, 'why aren't you already gone for that priest, Caleb?'

Twelve ecstatically happy months was all they'd had together, before the flush on her cheeks became more feverish, and a cough that began as a niggle quickly became a harsh bark.

'Tubercolosis,' the town doctor had confirmed. 'The curse of the Irish.'

Doc Fellows had recommended rest and mountain air. But all the rest and mountain air that Bridie could get, wasn't remedy enough. Within the year she was dead — mere skin and bone at the end when she died in his arms.

He had buried her in the mountains, and had ridden away, bereft, on a trail that had become persistently more wayward, until Tom Watson's letter had offered him the hope he had been seeking.

He recognized a landmark from Tom Watson's map — a jutting rock that Tom had described as a bald man with a lump on his head. Caleb Ross laughed on seeing the rock with the smaller rock on top, and reckoned that Tom's description was apt.

'Up ahead the road should fork, Belle,' Ross said to his horse, with whom he had had many conversations on the long and lonely trails he had ridden since Bridie's death.

About a half-mile on it was as Tom had said. An off-shoot trail to the right would take him directly to Ghost Creek. As he rode along, happy as a bee collecting pollen, Ross took in the rich pasture he was passing through.

'Cow country sure enough, Tom,' was his opinion of the flat countryside that ran to black-faced hills to the east which would, in winter, give shelter from storms.

The hills had stands of timber with bare stretches in between. Ross figured that the bare stretches were where homesteaders and ranchers had cut the lumber to build their houses. But there was plenty left, if Tom Watson had not already taken his share. The baring of the hills bothered him though. Without the controlling impediment that the trees would have provided, winter rains would flow swiftly off the hills, and if Tom had not already done so, the digging of drains and water-runs would be an immediate priority. The pattern of the felling suggested that if Ghost Creek was close by, Ghost Creek could be in line for most of the wash off the hills. Which meant that the early settlers in the area had cut lumber from parts of the hill from where the rains would not cascade down on their properties. Flooded pasture could very well be their lot for long stretches of winter and spring, if the drains and water-runs were not ready to trap and direct the flow.

Caleb Ross was not too worried. Tom Watson was above all else a planner. And he'd have long before now seen the danger from the denuded hills.

Rounding a bend in the trail, Ross saw a creek. The sun slanting through the willows covering its banks shimmered on the water, making the creek look like a stream of sparkling diamonds. He drew rein to let the mare drink and cool herself, before climbing the far bank from where, if Tom Watson's outlined ambitions had been fulfilled, he should be able to see his cabin.

Cresting the rise out of the creek he was looking into a bowl-shaped basin, at the southern end of which stood a sturdy cabin built back against a hill which, in winter, warmed by a wood-burning stove would be cozy, protected as it was by the hill and the curved shape of the landscape.

'El Dorado sure enough,' Caleb Ross told the mare. 'Tom,' he hailed as he got closer to the cabin. 'You home? It's Caleb Ross.'

There was no response. He hailed again and got the same result. He dismounted and hitched his horse to the rail outside the cabin.

'Tom?' he called, before pushing in the cabin door.

Caleb Ross stood stock-still in the open door. Well, that was what a man with any sense did when he was looking down the barrels of a primed shotgun.

3

'You say,' the man in the cripple's chair threatening him with the blaster said. 'But how do I know you're Caleb Ross?'

'I don't take kindly to being on the shooting end of a shotgun, friend,' Ross said, coldly.

'Tough!' the cripple barked. 'You got any proof that you're Ross? If you have, you'd best show it in the next coupla seconds.'

'I'll talk to Tom,' Ross said, annoyed by the continued threat of the shotgun.

'Ain't here.' The cripple raised the shotgun a notch. 'Proof or eternity, mister. The choice is yours to make.'

Grudgingly, Caleb Ross showed the cripple Tom Watson's letter.

'No darn good,' he said. 'Can't read.'

'I'll read it for you.'

'No darn good either.'

'Why not?'

''Cause what you're spoutin' might not be what you're readin'.'

'I'll read it anyway,' Caleb Ross said, grimly.

'It's your breath you'll be wastin',' the cripple said.

'Not a trusting fella, are you,' Ross said.

'Only a fool trusts round here, mister,' the other stated bluntly. 'This valley's got more vipers than blades of grass!'

Ross read the letter.

'Guess that's good enough,' the cripple said. He lowered the blaster. 'Them's words Tom would spout, sure 'nuff.' His gaze travelled over Caleb Ross. 'Gotta lotta dust on ya.'

'I've come a long way,' Ross said.

'Sorry 'bout this,' he slapped the shotgun, 'but these are troubled times. A man's got to be sure that he ain't lettin' a wolf in sheep's clothin' in the house. Where d'ya hail from?'

'Here and there,' Ross said.

'Saddlebum, huh!' The cripple grated.

'You're a hard man to like, mister,' Caleb Ross said.

'Likin' me or not ain't important. What's important is that when Tom comes back, this place'll be as he left it.'

'Troubled times, you said?' Ross questioned.

'With a capital T, Ross,' the cripple confirmed.

'That's not what Tom says here.' Ross waved Tom Watson's letter of hope and promise in the air. 'Heck, I figured that I was riding into heaven.'

'How old is that darn letter?'

'It took a spell to find me,' Ross admitted. 'Been chasing me around for most of a year.'

'That's a hell of a long time, mister,' the cripple said. 'Plenty's changed in a year. This valley ain't as hospitable as Tom wrote ya.'

'What's the problem?'

'Trouble's come in the shape of a fella called Scott Rawl, and his snake-in-the-grass sidekick Jack Sweeney. Poisonous as a rattler, is Sweeney. Hang 'round and it won't take long to cross paths with those trouble-stirring bastards. And bein' a friend of Tom's will make you real interestin' to them.'

'I've already met the gents,' Caleb Ross said.

'Yeah?' the cripple's eyes flashed interest. 'How come?'

Ross told the cripple about his brush with Scott Rawl and Jack Sweeney at the creek where he had stopped to fill his canteen.

'You're darn lucky to be still exercisin' your lungs,' the cripple said. 'Buckin' Rawl is a mighty dangerous thing to do.' He looked with a new respect at Caleb Ross. 'Brave, too.' Then he chuckled. 'As well as downright loco, o' course.'

He stuck out his right hand.

'Eli Scanell's the name, friend.'

Caleb Ross shook the cripple's hand. 'Is Tom out on the range?'

Scanell's eyes shadowed over.

'No, he ain't,' he said angrily. 'Took

off to town a couple o' days 'go. Pinin' for the company of a widder-woman he knows. Spins his senses, she does.'

Ross grinned. 'Tom was always a sucker for a petticoat. Guess he hasn't changed much since I last saw him.'

'I told him,' Eli Scanell complained. 'Told him good, too.'

'Told him what?'

'That it was dangerous goin' to town with trouble stalkin' this devil's range, until the boundaries are settled and the feudin's done. Don't do to stray round here. But d'ya think he'd listen to old busted-up Eli Scanell.'

The cripple was shaking his head, fit to come off his shoulders.

'Not by a long shot. Stubborn cuss, is Tom Watson. The devil's kin — Rawls,' he stated. Then with keen interest, he enquired: 'Did ya give Rawl back his water?'

'No.'

'Flat out you told him no?'

'Flat out,' Ross confirmed.

Once his satisfaction was spent, Eli

Scanell's craggy face clouded with worry.

'That makes you as close to a dead man as don't matter,' he warned. 'Borrowed time, that's what you're on, Ross.' He shook his shiny bald head, his demeanour dour. 'No one bucks a Rawl 'round here and stays 'bove ground for long. That's mighty costly water you've got in your canteen.'

'Has Tom locked horns with the Rawls?' Ross queried.

''Most every day.'

'How come he's still alive, if bucking the Rawls is as deadly as you say it is?'

'That's a question I've been askin' m'self for a long time. Haven't found an answer yet. Luck, I guess,' he concluded thoughtfully. 'But of late Tom's asked a lot of Lady Luck, and I keep tellin' him that there can't be much luck left to draw on. But he figures that sooner or later the Rawls will accept that he's in the valley to stay, and the trouble between them will end.'

'But you don't figure so?' Ross

42

quizzed the cripple.

'I seen the kind of bad blood that's 'tween Tom and Scott Rawl afore. And, like a boil, it'll keep right on festerin' until it breaks and the poison is released. You know what I think, Ross?'

'I'd sure like to hear,' Ross encouraged.

'I reckon that one of that pair will have to die. You've locked horns with Scott Rawl. He's a viper, that one.'

'Sarah Rawl seems to have him on a leash. And I reckon that she's not got her brother's venom.'

'Looks like Sam Rawl, Scott and Sarah's pa, has lost interest in cows and spends most of his time now chasing a career in Washington politics. Old man Rawl's absence has given Scott Rawl free rein.'

'Seems to me that Sarah Rawl is the bosslady?' Ross said. 'Kind of took me by surprise, I can tell you.'

'When he hightailed it to Washington, old man Rawl handed the reins to Sarah, her bein' older than Scott, until

Scott Rawl stepped from boy to man. And, up to the day that Jack Sweeney was hired, things worked just fine. But under Sweeney's poisonous influence, Scott Rawl's got bigger in his boots every day, and the leash Sarah had him on is getting more and more stretched. And I figure that, sooner rather than later, Scott Rawl will slip that leash completely.

'When that happens, the grass in this valley will run red. Ain't just room 'nuff in this valley for Scott Rawl and Tom Watson. Rawl's other neighbours, too. Even if they're dumbheaded 'nuff to think that by sayin' or doin' nothin' Scott Rawl will let 'em be.'

'What started the trouble?' Caleb Ross asked.

'Don't take much to start a feud in these parts. A coupla months back, Tom got the idea that he'd round up wild horses in a canyon near the Rawl ranch and break them. Never knowed a man who can talk to horses like Tom can — a real ace whisperer, is Tom Watson.'

Caleb Ross agreed. He had witnessed Tom Watson's affinity with horses time and again, and had been in awe of his friend's gift for horse-cajoling.

'Tom could always talk a horse in to what he wanted it to do,' Ross said.

'Pure horse-witchery,' Scanell said. 'There was a trader comin' to town. Tom figured that roundin' up the horses would be easy money to stash in the bank as a sign of his hard work and worthiness for the bank to give him a mortgage. But Scott Rawl reckoned that the horses should have been in the Rawl corral, though he never showed any interest in them until Tom decided to round them up. And that's where the bad blood 'tween Tom and Scott Rawl began. And ever since it's been getting blacker and more poisoned.

'Scott Rawl called on Tom. Told him that he had come to collect *his* horses. Tom ran him off under threat of a blunderbuss.

'At first, Tom's neighbours saw the right of his claim and took his side in the dispute. But when barns began catching fire without any good cause, and wells were spoiled in the dead of night, the trouble with the Rawls got too big a T for their likin', and,' his sneer was one of utter contempt, 'they back-slided and took to lickin' Scott Rawl's boots and kissin' his backside every chance they got. That left Tom on his own to face Rawl's might and spite.

'Tom never blamed no one. He knew that, like him, his neighbours were strugglin' to keep body and soul together, and they could not afford to give offence to the Rawls.

'Next thing, even though he sold the horses for a good price, the bank came up with every excuse in the book to deny Tom a mortgage. Rawl dollars stuffed the bank's coffers, and Sam Rawl made it clear that none of those dollars was to find its way to Tom Watson's pockets.

'But Tom turned every darn stone in heaven and hell to get the ranch up and running. And starting out with the money he got for the horses, he hauled supplies from Danesville, that's a town 'bout fifteen miles east of here, where the Rawls hold no sway.

'Flattened the shack he had been livin' in, and built this fine cabin. Gave up on talkin' to the Rawls about settlin' boundaries, and strung his fences. There was no chance that Scott Rawl would accept the boundaries, him wantin' the Rawl name on ev'ry inch o' pasture.'

The cripple's sigh was long and weary.

'Scott Rawl swore that if he ever caught Tom with a toe on Rawl range, he'd treat him no better than one of his darn cows. Sarah Rawl tried valiantly to cleanse the bad blood 'tween Tom and her brother. But with Jack Sweeney whisperin' in his ear, sense and reason had long deserted Scott Rawl.'

The cripple shook his head in wonder.

'Darnest thing for Sam Rawl to do an'way, makin' Sarah the bosslady. No man's goin' to kowtow to a petticoat.' Scanell snorted. 'So every Rawl hand would nod when Sarah Rawl gave an order, and then check with Scott Rawl before actin' on it.

'Sam Rawl should have handed over to Randy Dodd until Scott was ready. Dodd was the best darn ramrod in the territory. But he hightailed it when Sam Rawl went to Washington, and left him to take orders from a,' Scanell sneered, '*woman*. And be a nursemaid to a boy.'

Eli Scanell groaned.

'That's when Sarah started droppin' by to ask Tom for his counsel, her not bein' sometimes sure if her orders were as cock-eyed as the hands were claimin' they were. Tom should have sent her packin', told him so right then and there. But if it's one big flaw Tom Watson's got, it's his gentlemanly way when a woman comes a-calling.

'All it did was rile Scott Rawl all the more, when Tom gave Sarah Rawl counter arguments as to why things could not be done the way she wanted them done. Rawl came round one day, spitting more fire than a demon with indigestion, and called Tom out. Tom laughed off Rawl's challenge, and did the darnest most stupid thing he had done up to that. He turned his back on Scott Rawl.'

The cripple slapped his useless legs.

'I got 'tween Tom and Rawl. Took a bullet in the back.'

'If Scott Rawl backshot you, why isn't he breaking rocks?' Caleb Ross asked.

''Cause he's Scott Rawl,' the cripple said bitterly. ''Cause he's got a pa who'll be a senator after the fall elections. And 'cause Scott Rawl's got Dan Bennett in his pocket.'

'Dan Bennett?'

'The Ghost Creek marshal. Town took its name from the creek here. Of a kind with Jack Sweeney, is Bennett.'

The cripple looked at Caleb Ross. 'Are you any good with that iron on your hip?'

'It knows its way out of leather,' Ross said.

'Fast?'

'Most of the *hombres* who wanted to find out, aren't around,' Ross confirmed.

Scanell laughed.

'You know, Ross. You might be just what's needed round here.'

'I'm not a gunnie, Eli,' Ross said.

'But you shoot when you have cause, don't ya?'

Caleb Ross nodded.

'Well, you'll sure have cause after buckin' Scott Rawl and Jack Sweeney.' He considered Caleb Ross. 'Tom's been lookin' to the trail every day to see if you're ridin' in. Said that when you did, all the guff you two talked on those dusty cattle-drives wouldn't be just guff any more. Welcome to Fat Belly Ranch, Caleb Ross.'

'Fat Belly Ranch!' Ross yelped.

'There was no talkin' Tom Watson out of it,' Eli Scanell said. 'I near wore my tonsils out tryin'.'

Caleb Ross shook his head. 'Good grief,' he exclaimed. 'Fat Belly Ranch!'

Their laughter was interrupted by the thunder of approaching riders.

'Step aside!' Eli Scanell ordered.

Caleb Ross did as the fired-up cripple had ordered. Scott Rawl rode in with the men he had tangled with at the creek and a dozen more.

'Hold it right there, Rawl!' Eli Scanell bellowed with lungs that no one would suspect the smallish cripple of having. 'I kill vermin on sight.'

'Shut your mouth, cripple!' a man riding alongside Scott Rawl shouted.

The shotgun exploded. Caleb Ross felt the heat of its load blast past him. The man who had insulted Eli was lifted out of his saddle and tossed in the air like a sliver of straw in a winter storm, before he crashed to the ground, a bloodied parcel.

4

The drawback with a blaster, once triggered, is that it's pretty useless unless a fella is near enough to crack a skull with it. However, when faced with a dozen gun-toting riders, the shotgun's possible use as a cudgel doesn't arise. Then all a sensible fella is left with is a hasty retreat. Caleb Ross dived to the side of the cabin door, hauling Eli Scanell with him. The crippled man crashed helplessly to the floor.

'Kill the bastards!' Scott Rawl ordered angrily.

The riders with Rawl proved themselves eager to oblige. Bullets spat through the open cabin door and smashed through the window just above Ross, blasting shards of glass across and around the cabin, each missile as deadly as a stiletto.

'Damn murderin' bastards!' Scanell

raged, trying to crawl to the table where a rifle lay.

Caleb Ross grabbed him by the legs and pulled him back as close to the cabin wall as he could get. A bullet spun off a cooking-pot hanging above the stove and thudded into the cabin wall a mere sliver of an inch away from Ross's head.

The lead kept coming, ripping chunks of wood from the walls and wreaking havoc on crockery and utensils. The stovepipe had so many holes in it that it finally bent and collapsed.

'You goin' to cower all day?' Eli Scanell demanded to know of Ross. 'Like a snivelling no-good coward.'

'What good will it do to get shot full of holes?' Ross flung back.

The cripple snorted. 'Hah! They'll fill you full of holes anyway. Might as well go down fightin'.'

He struggled to break free, but Caleb Ross held him firm.

'Hold it!'

Scott Rawl's order was barely audible

above the thunder of guns, which by now must have melting barrels, Ross reckoned. The guns were silenced, and the silence left in their thunderous wake was even louder.

'I figure they've got more holes in 'em than we can count, Mr Rawl,' a man said gleefully.

'Wait!' Rawl shouted as a man moved forward.

'Don't even breathe,' Caleb Ross told Scanell.

'Ed's right,' another man said. 'No one could be left suckin' air in that cabin, Mr Rawl.'

'No point in finding out that we're wrong,' Scott Rawl barked. 'Larry . . . '

'Yes, Mr Rawl,' a man asnswered.

'Get that drum of kerosene near that shed over there.'

On hearing and guessing what Rawl's next move would be, the blood in Caleb Ross's veins froze.

'Douse the porch,' Rawl ordered.

'They're going to burn us out,' Eli Scanell said, fear stalking his eyes.

'Clever fella, Rawl,' Ross observed. 'Figures that if we're still alive, that once the fire gets going we'll run. If we don't we're fried meat. He wins either way.'

'What're we goin' to do, Ross?' Scannell asked anxiously.

'Well,' Ross said, crouching under the shattered window, 'I guess we shoot the fella with the drum of kerosene first.'

'And after that?'

Caleb Ross looked steadily at Eli Scanell. 'Are you a praying man, Eli?'

'Only when I have to.'

Ross thumped back the hammer of his sixgun.

'I reckon now is a *have to* time, friend,' he said, his tone grim.

Larry was uncapping the drum of kerosene when he paused for a second trying to figure out why he had a feeling of floating, before the bullet which had gone between his eyes spewed his brain out through the back of his head. As he fell backwards, his right leg shot out with the force of nerves jerking for the last time. His foot shot against the drum of kerosene, and the cap, almost off, sprang clear as the drum hit the hard ground. Kerosene gushed from the drum, spilling in the direction of the Rawl riders. Grasping an opportunity he had not expected to be presented with, Caleb Ross took advantage of the surprising turn of events to send two quick shots into the drum. The drum, ruptured by the hot lead, exploded in a ball of flame which raced along the snaking lines of spilled kerosene at an alarming rate. A rider not far from where Larry had fallen was thrown when his horse reared on seeing the trail of burning kerosene. He grabbed at the closest rider to break his fall. In his attempt to shrug him off, the second man also tumbled from his mount, and both men were pitched on to the flames. Several lines of burning kerosene linked up to trap the men. As the flames engulfed them, their cries for help went unheeded. The stench of burning flesh was gut-wrenching, as the men dropped, blackened scarecrows.

The Rawl crew danced their horses every which way in an attempt to avoid the unpredictable tracks of fire which were dictated by the fickle contours of the yard. Disorganized and panicked, they were easy targets for Ross's gun and two more men fell to his lead.

Good and bad luck jostled with each other. Burning kerosene had also splashed on to the cabin porch, and the tinder-dry wood was burning fiercely. Ross could not sit back and wait as he had planned, picking off the Rawl riders in their chaos, because in no time at all the flames would reach the cabin walls and race up them.

The cabin was set back into a hill, the purpose of which would be protection from winter storms and also to preserve heat inside the cabin. The drawback was that that left the cabin without a back door, making it necessary for Ross to leave the cabin by the front door, to face Rawl guns. Right now confusion gripped the Rawl bunch, but once they got sight of him the desire for revenge would override all other emotions. He was faced with a choice that was no choice at all. He could remain inside the cabin and burn alive. Or he could face Rawl gunfire. And added to his woes was the problem of Eli Scanell. The cripple could not help himself, so it was down to him to rescue Scanell.

'You'll have enough to do to try and save your own hide, Ross,' the crippled man said on understanding Caleb Ross's dilemma.

'Where I go, you go, Eli,' Ross stated doggedly.

'Don't talk crazy talk!' Scanell said tetchily. 'I'll be chairbound for the rest of my natural, and that ain't no life at all.'

Eli Scanell fixed Caleb Ross with a bleak stare.

'Tom will need your help to make the Fat Belly ranch, which don't amount to nothin' yet, a hard fact of life. So don't rob Tom of his dream by stupid chivalry. You get outta here while those

Rawl bastards are jumpin' in their skins.'

Caleb Ross shook his head.

'We go together, Eli,' he stated, hard-faced.

5

'In that case, best you take the rifle,' said Eli, unable to persuade Caleb Ross to let him be. 'I'll use your sixgun. Shoot as straight as a man bein' dragged can.'

Ross quickly replaced the spent bullets in the sixgun and handed it to Eli Scanell. 'You ready, Eli?'

'Ya know this is loco, Ross,' Scanell said in one final attempt at persuading Ross to abandon him.

'Eli Scanell,' Caleb Ross said determinedly, 'get one thing through your mule head. You, me and Tom Watson are going to build the Fat Belly ranch together. So stop your grousing and start your shooting!'

He crouched down. 'Get on my back, Eli.'

'On your back?'

'Better than trying to drag you with me.'

Ross helped the crippled man on to his back and straightened up, puffing. 'You ain't exactly been starving yourself, have you, Eli.'

'Let's hope that I've got 'nuff gut-fat to absorb flyin' lead,' Eli chortled.

Ross collected the rifle from the table, and then went to the cabin door.

'Grab my shoulder with one hand and shoot as fast as you can with the other,' he instructed the crippled man.

Ross opened the cabin door a fraction.

'When I yank this door open, start shooting and don't stop until you've got no bullets left or you're dead, Eli!'

Caleb Ross put every smidgen of energy he had into his leg muscles to give him the impetus he'd need once he opened the cabin door. He recalled a horse-trough to the left of the door, and that was where he was headed.

'Makes sense, Caleb,' Scanell agreed when Ross told him.

Ross tensed, took a couple of deep breaths, and steadied himself to get his balance right. The last thing he'd want was to misjudge the crippled man's weight and fall over.

'Wait!' Scanell advised, nodding as smoke rolled across the front of the cabin. 'Another coupla seconds and that smoke will be as thick as molasses.'

Flame flashed through the window near the door, leaping towards them, almost taking them by surprise. Scanell grimaced as the tip of the tongue of flame licked his left arm.

'We don't have seconds left,' Ross said. 'Time to teach that Rawl bunch a lesson, Eli.'

'Teach 'em good too, friend,' Scanell said, and added with genuine warmth: 'I'd have liked to have known you a spell longer, Ross.'

'They'll be lots of time in the future to get to know each other real well, Eli.'

Scanell cocked the sixgun.

'Yank that damn door open, Caleb!' he said grimly. 'And let's sling lead at those Rawl bastards!'

Fortunately for them, the confusion

caused by the spreading inferno outside the house, which had by now set fire to brush and scrub in a circle around the Rawl outfit, handed Caleb Ross and Eli Scanell an advantage. Their sudden emergence from the cabin, guns blasting, added to the Rawl riders' confusion. Several men dropped from their saddles into the flames. Scott Rawl and Jack Sweeney were quickest to react, and their bullets ripped chunks from the horse-trough as Caleb Ross dived behind it, Eli Scanell's weight sending him down heavily. The impact with the hard ground was punishing, and the force and helplessness of his dive dislodged Scanell from his back and pitched him beyond the horse-trough on to open ground. He lay on the ground, cruelly exposed to the deadly threat of Scott Rawl's gun. The evil scowl on Rawl's face was devoid of all mercy.

Eli Scanell was a dead man.

Forcing the pain of his crunching fall aside, Caleb Ross curled his gunhand round the side of the water-trough at Scott Rawl.

'Freeze!'

Ross stiffened.

'Got him cold, Mr Rawl,' the man said. 'Want me to finish him off?'

6

Caleb Ross cursed his lack of foresight in underestimating Scott Rawl's canniness. He had figured him to be ninety-nine per cent brawn and one per cent brain. It had now proved to be a costly miscalculation. Rawl had not been stupid enough to think that all he'd have to do was ride up and flush out the occupants of the cabin. He had, by positioning a man to the rear of the cabin, taken a wise precaution against fickle chance, which had now worked in his favour.

'No,' Rawl barked, in answer to the man's offer to finish Ross off. 'I'll reserve that pleasure for myself, Hank.'

'Mebbe you should just toss him back in the fire,' Hank suggested.

'Maybe that's a good idea,' Rawl laughed. 'But first . . . ' He drew a bead on Eli Scanell. 'Crawl, cripple!'

'See you in hell, Rawl,' Eli Scanell flung back.

'Leave him be, Rawl,' Caleb Ross interceded. 'He's a helpless cripple. It's me you really want.'

'The deadleg's been quite a thorn in my side, Ross,' Rawl said. 'Never let a chance to stir trouble for the Rawl brand go by. I'd have dispatched him a long time ago, only my old man, now that he figures that one day he'll be president,' his tone was scoffing, 'lost his grit for settling things in the way he used to. By gun and rope.'

'Maybe your pa understands that with law and order coming to the territories, it's time to hang up the guns and throw away the ropes, before the new breed of lawman will deliver the justice such deeds deserve.'

Scott Rawl was dismissive of any such idea.

'No lawman would dare touch a Rawl!'

With such dumbhead thinking, Ross reassessed his opinion of Scott Rawl, and reckoned that maybe after all, his first impressions were right and Rawl was indeed ninety-nine per cent brawn and one per cent brain, and had only got it right this once when he had taken the precaution of putting Hank behind the cabin.

'Mighty oaks have fallen to new winds before,' Caleb Ross said, sagely.

'If you don't dispatch this critter soon, boss,' Hank said. 'I reckon he'll just run outta breath and die of fright.'

Rawl laughed. 'Yeah, I guess you just might be right at that, Hank.'

Caleb Ross stood up, swayed, put a hand to his forehead, staggered and crumpled.

'Shit,' Hank swore. 'I do believe that Ross has fainted like a petticoat, Mr Rawl.'

'Get him up!' Rawl barked.

Caleb Ross heard words he'd been praying he'd hear. Hank leaned over to do as his boss had ordered, and was a mightily surprised man when he saw Ross's wide grin, before his knee came up to pulverize Hank's groin.

Howling, and dancing a credible Irish jig, Hank was too concerned with his own pain to be any further threat to Ross, or use to Rawl. Ross sprang up and grabbed the hapless Rawl man to use as a shield, just in time for him to stop Scott Rawl's bullet. Aware of how big a target he made astride his horse, Scott Rawl threw himself from the stallion into nearby brush to break the impact of his fall. However, what seemed a good idea at first, turned out not to be so good as he became entangled in the thick scrub. By the time he disentangled himself, Caleb Ross had him firmly under threat from his Winchester.

'Anyone as much as twitches an eyelid and your boss is dead,' Ross warned the remaining Rawl men, who had just about got themselves into some kind of order.

'What d'ya want we should do, Mr Rawl?' a small runtish man asked.

Scott Rawl's eyes flashed between

Caleb Ross and the men, swiftly assessing his chance of survival, should they open fire on Ross.

'You'll be in hell before me, Rawl,' Ross promised icily.

'Boss?' the runtish man pressed, obviously to the displeasure of the other men.

They knew by now that in Caleb Ross they had a formidable and fast-thinking adversary, and that they were not dealing with the normal scared honcho they usually tormented.

'Your call, Rawl,' Caleb Ross said grimly.

Scott Rawl swallowed hard, and his eyes became haunted.

'You'd better clear out of this neck of the woods pronto, Ross!' he declared fierily, putting the best face he could on his withdrawal.

Though sorely tempted, Ross resisted adding to Scott Rawl's humiliation by emphasizing his supremacy. However, he did state unequivocally:

'I plan to stay put, Rawl.' And then

he added placatingly: 'I want us to be good neighbours. Our differences are now behind us, I hope.'

'Go to hell!' Scott Rawl fumed. Mounted up, he declared: 'You should have killed me when you had the chance, Ross. I'll kill you if I get the chance.'

He swung the stallion and galloped away, followed by his men, eager to be free from the threat of the grim reaper's finger selecting them.

'Rawl's right!' Eli Scanell growled. 'You are a fool, Ross. You should have killed him when you had the chance.'

Caleb Ross considered the cripple. 'Someone's got to silence his gun first for peace to take hold, Eli.'

'You've got a hole in your head the width of the Grand Canyon, if you think Scott Rawl will rest until he's buried you, friend.'

The crash of the cabin's collapsing roof got their attention.

'And Tom's going to be as mad as a

coyote at full moon, Ross!'

Caleb Ross's shoulders slumped wearily. It seemed that his arrival in Ghost Creek had only added to Tom Watson's stack of troubles.

7

Sarah Rawl paced the den casting furious glances at her brother, who glared back truculently, unfazed by his older sibling's smouldering anger which, only a year ago, would have had him repentant. However, that year had made all the difference in his attitude. As Scott Rawl saw it, he had gone from boy to man and was now the rightful boss of Rawl range and interests.

'The trouble has to stop, Scott,' Sarah commanded. 'First you pick a fight with Tom Watson for no good reason, and now you've got Ross on our backs.'

'I don't feel nothing on my back, sis!' Rawl flung back.

'Then you're a bigger fool than I thought you were, Scott,' she said, contemptuously. 'Crowding Tom Watson and ratcheting up trouble with Ross isn't the same thing.'

Rawl scoffed. 'Hah! Ross don't scare me none.'

'That shows the kind of fool you are,' Sarah Rawl threw back. 'Watson blusters, a lot of wind and hothead talk. But Ross is different, Scott. He'll do as he says he'll do, and you can count on that. Stay out of his way!' she commanded.

'Is that an order, bosslady?' Scott sneered.

'That's exactly what it is, Scott,' she confirmed. 'When Pa took off for Washington he saw fit to hand me the responsibility of looking after what he had built. I didn't want the job, and I told him so, but he went ahead anyway. So I'm obliged to see that when he comes home, Rawl affairs will be as he left them or better.

'And when he does come home, I'll be only too eager to hand him back the reins and return to what I truly love, being a teacher.'

'Pa didn't do right by me, putting

you in charge,' Rawl grumbled. 'It ain't fitting for a skirt to be the boss of a ranch.'

'Jack Sweeney's opinion, is it?' Sarah charged, angrily. 'Oh, Scott,' she pleaded, her anger gone as soon as it had flashed, 'Sweeney isn't any fit friend for you — for any man. Jack Sweeney is the dregs of the dregs, Scott.'

'I pick my own friends, Sarah,' he growled.

'Look, Scott, I know Pa would have wished that you were the first born, but you weren't. And those six years between us is what prompted Pa to put the load on my shoulders. He called those years calming years; the years between boy and man in which sense and good judgement are acquired.'

'I'm not a boy, Sarah!' Scott Rawl raged.

'If that's so, then stop acting like one,' she tossed back, the leash on her patience slipping. 'Go back to Ross and accept his offer of reconcilation. And tomorrow get a crew together to cut and haul lumber to rebuild what you burned down! And it's also time to stop locking horns with Tom Watson.'

'Why the hell don't you just go back to teaching snotty-nosed brats and leave the ranch to me!'

Sarah Rawl laughed sadly.

'God, Scott, how I wish I could do just that.'

'There's nothing to it. I'll even saddle your horse.' He scowled darkly. 'The only finger I'm going to lift to help Ross, is my trigger finger, sis,' he said dourly.

'Then I'll be burying you for sure, if you try, brother,' Sarah Rawl said, with a deathbed sigh.

★　★　★

The subject of the talk at the Rawl ranch house was in the process of settling in with Eli Scanell to the temporary abode of the rotting shack further along Ghost Creek which Tom

75

Watson had lived in before he had built the cabin.

'The damn place was finished only a week when I got a bullet in my back,' Scanell said, as they viewed the smouldering debris of the cabin.

'Tom and me will have a new cabin built before you can spit, Eli,' was Caleb Ross's promise.

The cripple's eyes clouded over.

'Ain't goin' to be the same,' he said, soulfully. 'Never is, a new abode. Those cabin walls listened to me and Tom gab on endlessly about when you would put in an appearance, and how the three of us together would build the finest ranch 'tween here and the end of the earth. An ocean of cows chompin' grass so green that an Irish shamrock would hide in shame.'

A wave of guilt washed over Caleb Ross, which made him keenly regretful that he had ever set foot in Ghost Creek. Had he ignored his friend's letter and stuck to his footloose ways, Tom Watson would still have his fine cabin and would probably eventually come to terms of settlement with the Rawls. He suspected that Sarah Rawl already saw the sense of peaceful and neighbourly living. He reckoned that it showed in her eagerness to assuage her brother's anger back at the creek. And, add another year or so to Scott Rawl and he'd probably also settle down, once his transition from boy to man was completed. And all his presence had achieved was the likely postponement of the day when the Fat Belly ranch and the Rawl ranch would establish peaceful relations to the prosperity of both.

'You're figurin' that you should never have come, ain't ya?' Eli Scanell asked, with shrewd insight.

'Well, fact is, Eli,' Caleb Ross groaned, 'that I've stirred up a hornet's nest for you and Tom.'

'If you think that, your brain ain't as fast as your gun hand, that's for sure. You're thinkin' right now that if you hadn't put in an appearance the trouble 'tween Tom and Rawl would settle.'

The cripple shook his head. 'No chance, Ross. Their horns are locked and will remain locked until one of them expires. It surely has shaped up to be a fight to the end. At least now, Tom's got someone who can shoot straight. Never knowed why Tom Watson packed a gun. Couldn't hit the side of a barn from ten damn feet away. Told him more'n once that all packin' an iron did for him was attract trouble that couldn't be solved without pistols spittin'. That sooner or later sportin' a gun would get him into the kind of gun trouble that he couldn't get out of.'

He laughed reflectively.

'But there's no darn persuadin' him that he ain't the gun-slickest *hombre* this side of the Rio Grande!'

Recalling how every man on a cattle-drive ducked when Tom drew a sixgun, Caleb Ross laughed along with Eli Scanell.

'Every man's got a blind spot, Eli.' He chuckled.

'Not the size of the darn moon, they don't!'

Their laughter went on for a spell longer, giving welcome relief from the brooding depression which the encounter with Scott Rawl had left in its wake. When it died, Eli Scanell reassured Ross:

'The loss of the cabin will be forgotten in Tom's delight when he eventually sets his peepers on you, Caleb. Now we've got to make this shack as presentable and as habitable as possible. I can't help much in a cripple's chair.'

He looked round the shack, his nostrils pinched.

'Whichever of God's creatures have been using this place, sure shit a mountain! Darn critters.'

Several hours of broom and scrubber eventually got the shack into the best state that it could be restored to.

'Brush and scrub any more, and you'll remove the dirt that holds this place together,' Eli opined jokingly.

'And,' he brushed the air in front of him, 'you'd better go jump in the creek.'

Caleb Ross sniffed at himself and gagged.

'Guess that's the best idea you've had so far today, Eli.' He chuckled.

'We ain't got soap,' the cripple said. 'That's in the supplies that Tom should have been back with three days ago. I do swear that the Widow Flannery must have pleasures that a man would keep demandin' until he draws his last breath.'

Scanell took in Caleb Ross's grubby condition.

'Go jump in the creek. Maybe all that dirt on ya will poison a few Rawl cows.'

'Be back in no time at all, Eli,' Ross promised, departing. He handed him the rifle. 'You cut loose if you get any callers.'

Though it was late evening, the water of the creek still had the warmth of the day, and Ross let its gentle movement wash over him. The creek was full of the eerie shadows that exist between the setting of the sun and the rising of the moon. As he bathed, he kept changing direction to watch the shadows. Tempers from the hostile afternoon would still be frayed, and Ross was conscious of how inviting and how easy a target he was. A Rawl man who happened to pass by might decide to ingratiate himself with Scott Rawl by offing his new adversary. However, as time passed and no threat emerged, Ross relaxed.

And that was when it happened!

8

The dislodged pebble rolled down the hilly far bank of the creek and splashed into the water. Acting on instinct, Caleb Ross leapt out of the creek and scrambled for his sixgun on a nearby boulder. Not very hopeful that he'd make it to the weapon, he tensed against the bullet he expected in the back at any second. To his surprise he reached his gun and took cover behind the boulder, his eyes searching the far side of the creek for the lurker. With no sign of a two-legged critter, he considered that the pebble might have been dislodged by a four-legged predator. However, he quickly discounted a threat of a four-legged kind, because the creek was too intensely still. If it had been a coyote or another variety of wild creature, other smaller animals would be reacting to its presence, scurrying away to avoid ending up between its jaws. So if it wasn't a four-legged lurker, it had to be a two-legged one. And the two-legged variety would be by far the more dangerous.

'Show yourself, or I'll pepper that hill with lead,' Caleb Ross called out in warning. 'I'll count to three, then I'll start shooting.'

Nothing stirred.

'Have it your way, friend. One . . . Two . . . Thr — '

Sarah Rawl showed herself from behind a clutch of bushes.

'Good evening, Mr Ross,' she greeted. 'A mighty pleasant one too, isn't it.'

'Yeah. S-sure,' Ross stammered, suddenly recalling his all-revealing leap out of the water.

Apparently unconcerned, Sarah Rawl turned to follow a track along the edge of the creek to an exit further along. She paused and turned.

'Oh, by the way, you're bathing in

Rawl water, too.'

'In that case I must be sure not to drink it.' He chuckled. 'How long have you been watching?'

'You flatter yourself, Mr Ross. I come to the creek most evenings to remember better times.'

'Better times?'

'Yes. When the gentle soul who was my mother used to bring me here, and we'd talk and pick wild flowers for the fancy china vase in the parlour. And she'd try and ignore the sound of gunfire, as yet another dispute erupted over water and boundaries and pasture and cows,' she said, wearily.

'Seems not a whole lot's changed,' Ross observed drily.

'It had, until the rumpus between Tom Watson and Scott blew up.'

'Wild horses are any man's right to round up, ma'am.'

'I'm not denying that, Mr Ross.'

'Did you tell your brother that?'

Her weariness became hopelessness.

'A million times it seems,' she said.

'But the horses were only an excuse. I figure that the real reason for Scott's bitterness is a woman.'

'The Widow Flannery?'

Sarah Rawl was surprised by the extent of Caleb Ross's knowledge.

'You've picked up the neighbourhood gossip quickly,' she said, with a hint of rebuke.

'Your brother is not much more than a boy. Kind of young, I'd say, to be paying calls on a widow-woman,' Ross opined.

'I can see that your knowledge of the Widow Flannery is limited, Mr Ross. Kate Flannery is only twenty-two years old.'

'Twenty two!' Ross exclaimed. 'And a widow?'

'Married Alec Flannery only last year. He was a drunk. Picked a fight outside the saloon with a horse. The horse kicked him in the head.'

'But Tom is older than me by three years,' Ross exclaimed, 'and I ain't no spring chick.'

'There's no understanding these matters, is there,' Sarah Rawl said, in a worldly fashion. 'Oh, and, ah . . . I think your hat might come in handy, Mr Ross.'

'Huh?'

Suddenly Caleb Ross realized that he had stood up in astonishment on hearing the Widow Flannery's age.

' 'Night, Mr Ross.'

Sarah Rawl's laughter mocked him from the shadows.

*   *   *

Morning came peaceful and still. Acting on Eli Scanell's advice, Caleb Ross headed for town to rescue Tom Watson from the Widow Flannery's clutches.

'Tom must be thread-thin by now,' Eli said, grouchily. 'This is his third day in the Widow Flannery's bed.' He chuckled slyly. 'Goddam, some fellas've got all the luck!'

As Ross rode away, the cripple called: 'You be careful, Caleb. Don't look on that woman or you're finished, too. Or,' he chuckled, 'if the widow sees what Sarah Rawl saw, she mightn't just let you go.'

'You're a dirty old man, Eli Scanell,' Ross jokingly scolded him, regretting having told him about the incident at the creek the evening before. He'd surely relay it to Tom Watson, and he'd be longer in the tooth by a mile before they'd stop joshing him about it.

'No fun in bein' clean and bored, Ross,' Eli chortled.

It took Ross two hours to reach town, because he let his horse amble and eat the rich grass along the way. Besides, he did not want to walk in on Tom Watson too early. As he recalled, Tom was particularly passionate in the early morning. Besides, he was pleasurably thinking about Sarah Rawl. In fact his thoughts were a continuation of his dreams.

When he eventually reached town the citizens of Ghost Creek (the town had taken its name from the creek where

Tom's ranch was) were going about their business, visiting the stores and bank and gathering in groups talking and exchanging news and views. As towns went, Ghost Creek would be in the upper half of the league. Or maybe, Ross thought, it only looked that way because of the long periods of time he had in recent years spent in towns that were either dying or beginning and had either lost their sheen or had not yet got it. But Ghost Creek looked like the kind of town where a man could grow old in the company of good friends and neighbours. Some towns were like that. They drew you in. Others had no welcome, and were purely watering-hole stops along a trail that might, if a fella was lucky, end in a town like Ghost Creek.

As Ross rode by on his way to the white clapboard house at the south end of the main drag, the Widow Flannery's house, folk were beginning to pause on the boardwalks, and the chatter became muted as eyes went to a point behind

Ross. He turned in his saddle to see what was of such interest, and saw the funeral procession. Four men, astonishingly more drunk than sober, were staggering under the coffin they were carrying. Ross could only conclude that the drunks were burying one of their own kind in some strange ritual. Or perhaps the funds available were not sufficient to pay for a hearse. Whatever the reason, the wobbling pall-bearers made for strange viewing. And maybe, Caleb Ross began to think, that after all Ghost Creek might not be the kind of friendly town he had at first thought it was? Letting a man go to his grave in such a fashion was not the mark of a caring community.

Mulling over his thoughts, he rode on to the Widow Flannery's.

'Howdy ma'am,' he greeted the pretty woman who answered his knock. 'I was wondering if I might jaw with Tom.'

'Tom? Tom Watson you mean?'

'Yes, ma'am.'

Caleb Ross was at a loss to understand the widow's sudden anger.

'What kind of sick bastard are you?' she exploded.

Ross stepped back as the Widow Flannery lunged at him, her fists hammering on his chest. He grabbed her by the wrists to restrain her, but she fought him like a mountain cat. Eventually subdued, she began to weep in great gulping sobs. And now, on closer scrutiny, Ross could see that the widow's current sobbing was the tail-end of hours of weeping.

'I'm Tom Watson's friend, ma'am,' Ross informed the distraught woman. 'What seems to be the problem?'

'You're the friend Tom's been expecting for over a year now — Caleb Ross?'

'Yes, ma'am.'

The Widow Flannery began to weep again, but this time her tears were tears of sad reflection. 'Tom's been filling my head about how you and him were going to build the biggest ranch in the territory. And I kept telling him that you weren't going to show up. But he said,' she jutted her chin the way Tom did when his stubborn streak came to the fore, 'sure he will.' She mimicked Tom Watson. 'A tad late, true enough. But Caleb Ross will turn up sooner or later.'

The Widow Flannery's sad gaze went beyond Ross to the pitiful funeral cortège going past.

' 'Sooner or later,' Tom said, Mr Ross. But too late.'

Caleb Ross swung round to view the funeral procession, the drunks carrying the coffin wobbling under its weight and on their wayward legs. He swung back to face the Widow Flannery.

'Of late Tom got a fondness for liquor; a fondness I had persuaded him to let go. But last night, hurting as he was, I could not, despite my best efforts, keep Tom away from the saloon. And that's where he got into an argument with Jack Sweeney, a Rawl hardcase, always eager to stoke trouble. Tom foolishly took Sweeney's bait and was prodded in to drawing against him.

'Tom was no gunnie,' she said bitterly. 'Never stood a chance going up against Jack Sweeney.'

Caleb Ross was stunned to the roots of his hair. Arriving in Ghost Creek for Tom Watson's funeral was the cruelest blow fate had ever dealt him.

'Tom didn't have the shekels for a proper funeral with a hearse and a good coffin,' Kate Flannery said. 'Neither do I. And the only men Ed Blunt, the undertaker, could get to carry his coffin were a quartet of drunks from the saloon who were willing to perform the task for a bottle of rotgut each.'

'Well,' Caleb Ross declared, 'Tom will have one set of steady legs to shoulder him.' He studied the Widow Flannery. 'Ain't you going to the funeral, ma'am'?'

Kate Flannery shook her head.

'If you don't mind my saying so,' Ross stated bluntly. 'You not being there seems kind of disrespectful, ma'am. Tom caring for you so much, as

I understand from Eli Scanell.'

The Widow Flannery bowed her head.

'You're right of course, Mr Ross. I was only selfishly thinking of my own pain.'

'You said Tom was hurting, ma'am. Why?'

The Widow Flannery was about to answer Ross's question when she glared in horror beyond him. Ross swung around in time to see one of the pair of drunken pall-bearers at the front of the coffin stumble, and the coffin was pitched to the ground. The plain, slapped-together box in which Tom Watson rested, was not up to the impact and split open. Ross watched in horror as his friend's body rolled on to the dusty street and ended up face down in a mound of horse manure. There was a gasp of shock from those watching the cortège, most of whom had been standing in a respectful if curious silence. The exception was a handful of saloon rowdies, who had formed a mocking procession behind Tom's coffin, and who obviously thought that the incident was the funniest they had seen in a long time.

Kate Flannery's wail seemed to fill every inch of the street.

The drunks laughed all the more.

Fury replacing shock, Caleb Ross dashed into the street and scattered them under threat of his sixgun. He then picked up Tom Watson's remains and carried them to the Widow Flannery's house, where he laid them on a bed. The letter R within a circle, burned into Tom's left shoulder, visible through a tear in his shirt, got Ross's attention. He tore the material of the shirt more to get a full view of the awful wound, still crusted with dried blood and yellow pus.

'That's what Tom was hurting so badly from, Mr Ross.'

Caleb Ross turned to Kate Flannery in the doorway.

'That's the Rawl brand on Tom's shoulder,' she explained. 'Burned in with a Rawl branding-iron a couple of days ago, when Tom unwisely took a short cut to town across Rawl range.'

Though Caleb Ross had witnessed many cruel things in riding the trails of the West he had never heard of, or seen anything as cruel and demeaning as branding a man as cattle would be branded. A white-hot rage burned inside him.

'You sit with Tom,' he instructed Kate Flannery.

'Where're you headed?' she questioned him as Ross stormed from the room.

'First, to arrange for a decent burial for Tom. Then,' his face had the grimness of his seething anger, 'the Rawl ranch!'

9

Ed Blunt, the undertaker, came to meet Caleb Ross as, even more grim-faced, he bore down on the funeral parlour.

'Tom Watson was a charity case, mister,' he told Ross, anxiously, misinterpreting Ross's anger. 'I didn't get a darn cent.'

'My beef is not with you, undertaker,' Ross said.

'I'm surely glad to hear that, sir,' Ed Blunt said, relieved. 'And I'll deliver another box to bury Tom in, nothing fancy you understand. Just plain and simple.'

'Nothing wrong with a plain and simple box,' Ross said. 'God doesn't judge a man by what he's delivered in. But that doesn't say that the delivery has to be made without due respect to his creation.'

Caleb Ross held the undertaker's gaze.

'Tom Watson will go to his maker in a proper hearse with a preacher making the introduction.'

Ed Blunt shifted uneasily.

'Is that a problem?' Ross demanded to know.

'Well, put bluntly, you might say,' The undertaker smiled with quivering lips, keeping a keen eye on Ross for any sign of an adverse reaction. 'A hearse and preacher costs, mister.'

Caleb Ross dug into the pocket of his trousers and came up with a fistful of dollars that had the undertaker's eyes gleaming greedily. The stash was what was left of a successful poker session which Caleb had stopped off to join in, on his way to Ghost Creek, a stop-off which he now bitterly regretted making. Because if he had not delayed, he'd have arrived in Ghost Creek a week earlier, and Tom Watson would still be alive.

He handed the roll of bills to the undertaker.

'Peel off what the best funeral you

can provide costs,' he instructed Ed Blunt.

The undertaker gladly obliged, and added a couple of dollars more than was justified, before handing back the remainder of the stash to Ross.

'That it?'

'Yes, sir.' The undertaker's fingers felt the dollar bills. 'This will give Tom Watson the finest funeral this town's ever seen.'

'When?'

'Well . . .'

'I'm a man in a hurry, undertaker,' Ross stated.

'Say an hour?'

'Fine. Tom's remains are at Kate Flannery's.'

'I'll collect them right away,' Blunt said, eager to please a customer who had not argued about every last cent.

'I'll go on ahead,' Ross said.

'Yes, sir. Be there in five minutes,' Ed Blunt promised.

On his way back to Kate Flannery's house, Caleb Ross was the object of much curiosity. But no one barred his progress. In fact everyone was keen to step aside, as anyone would be who saw a scowling man bearing down on them. On arriving back at Kate Flannery's, he found the grieving woman sitting quietly holding Tom's hand, her face a mask of memories and regret at what might have been.

Ross stood quietly and respectfully at the bedroom door, allowing her the short time with Tom before the undertaker arrived. When Blunt put in an appearance with a preacher who read from the Bible while Tom Watson was being lowered into a handsome oak coffin, Ross offered his shoulder to Kate to weep on. Then he supported her on Tom Watson's final journey to his resting-place in the cemetery just outside town. Four sober and brawny pall-bearers bore Tom's coffin from the hearse to the grave. The preacher prayed while the coffin was being lowered into the soft black earth. That done, everyone including Ross, departed and stood off a respectful distance while Kate Flannery said her final farewell to the man she had so obviously loved. Then, the service finally over, and to the sound of earth crashing on to Tom Watson's coffin, Caleb Ross escorted Kate back to her house.

'Won't you stay awhile, Mr Ross?' she asked, when he immediately turned to leave.

'I'm a tad hurried, ma'am' he said.

'To avenge Tom's death?'

He nodded.

'And what will that achieve, Mr Ross?'

Caleb Ross studied Kate Flannery keenly.

'I'd say justice for Tom,' he growled. 'I figured that that's what you'd want too, ma'am!'

'I was in love with a fool, Mr Ross.' Caleb Ross was staggered by her blunt statement. 'Tom was every inch as big a fool as Scott Rawl is. He wouldn't listen to anyone. If Scott Rawl took a day off prodding, Tom would use that time to prod Rawl.

'Only a couple of weeks ago, Sarah Rawl sat right here in this parlour pleading with Tom to back off for a spell to give her time to work on her brother, in the hope that the feud between them could be ended.'

Kate Flannery shook her head sadly.

'Tom turned his face against any compromise. Told Sarah Rawl that he wouldn't budge an inch. That Scott would have to do any backing-off that was needed. Sarah reminded Tom that for an argument to end, someone had to have the courage to make the first move.'

She sighed wearily.

'I pleaded with Tom to give Sarah a chance to work on Scott. But I got as little out of my pleadings as Sarah Rawl had.

'Then Tom went and brazenly trespassed on Rawl range! Wasn't that the dumbest thing to do, Mr Ross? He handed Scott Rawl and that snot

Sweeney the chance they'd been angling for.'

Ross knew how Tom Watson's stubborn streak often blinded him to good sense, but instead of agreeing with Kate Flannery he had a question to ask, which, as far as he was concerned, needed asking right then and there.

'Scott Rawl was sweet on you, wasn't he?'

Kate Flannery nodded. 'But I was in love with Tom, and told Scott so.'

'About the time that Tom decided to round up those wild horses?' Ross quizzed.

'The day before.'

'That,' Caleb Ross said, 'explains a whole lot, ma'am.'

'Was all of this my fault, Mr Ross? All the bad blood, ending in Tom's death?'

Caleb Ross held Kate Flannery gently.

'No, it wasn't,' he said. 'You were just a woman in love who honestly said so.'

'Though I told Scott that I loved Tom Watson, it didn't stop him from coming round or accosting me in the street or from forcing his kisses on me that day Tom saw us at the creek on my way to visit with Tom. Tom laid into him, and the feuding between them just got worse.'

'And now that Tom's gone'?' Ross said.

'If you're asking if Scott Rawl will fill Tom's boots, the answer is no, Mr Ross.' She smiled sadly. 'The fact is that Scott Rawl, and indeed any other man of my acquaintance, could never hope to come near filling Tom Watson's boots. Does that answer your question, Mr Ross?'

'Without a doubt, ma'am,' he replied.

'Do you still intend to ride out to the Rawl ranch, Mr Ross?'

'Yes, I do,' he stated bluntly.

'Then you might very well be as big a fool as Tom was,' she said.

'Maybe,' Ross conceded.

On his way out of town, Ross's path was blocked by a burly, mean-eyed man.

'Dan Bennett's the name,' he said. 'I'm the law round here.' He turned back the flap of his vest to reveal a marshal's badge. 'I hear tell that you were a friend of Tom Watson. That right?'

'That was my privilege, Marshal,' Ross confirmed.

'Staying around long?'

'Haven't decided.'

'When will you be deciding?' Bennett pressed, his tone sharp to the point of confrontation.

'Can't say right now, Marshal,' Caleb Ross intoned.

'And when might you be able to say?'

Ross hunched his shoulders.

'When I've got an answer to your question.'

'Got a smart mouth, ain't ya?'

'I don't figure so, Marshal.'

'Yeah,' Bennett growled. 'Well, that's my opinion!'

'Every man's entitled to one — an opinion, I mean,' Ross drawled, refusing to be intimidated. 'You asked me a question which I don't have an answer to yet. When I have that answer I'll pass it along, Marshal.'

Ross went to ride on. Bennett grabbed his reins.

'Are you planning on taking up the trouble with Scott Rawl that Watson started?'

'I didn't hear it that way, Marshal. The story I heard was that the bad blood between Rawl and Tom began when Tom decided to round up some wild horses that were there for any man of a mind to do so.'

Marshal Dan Bennett scowled.

'That's not the way I heard it,' he stated gruffly.

'Who did you hear the story from, Marshal?'

'Scott Rawl.'

'And did you ask Tom Watson for his slant on Rawl's story?'

'Now why would I want to do that? Scott Rawl ain't no liar.'

'I reckon it would only have been fair to hear both sides of the argument,

Marshal,' Caleb Ross said, his tone tetchy.

Bennett stepped back a couple of paces, his right hand on his hip, inches from the Colt sixgun. 'Ya know, mister, that sounds like you're questioning my judgement?' His tone dropped an icy notch. 'And my honesty, too, I reckon.'

Caleb Ross shook his head.

'Only your fair-mindedness, Marshal,' he stated.

Bennett was clearly not used to backchat, and it was obvious that he thought that his hint at drawing iron would have been enough to have Ross back-tracking. His amazement was matched by the small group of increasingly interested onlookers who had gathered on the boardwalk outside the marshal's office.

'That a fact,' Bennett growled, aware of the acute interest his confrontation with the stranger was generating, and also the threat to his standing in the community should he allow himself to be browbeaten. He gave Ross an ultimatum. 'Step down from your horse, mister.'

'I'm not looking for a fight, Marshal,' Ross said. 'I'm just a man wanting to be on my way, and you're blocking my path. For no good reason that I can see.'

Bennett stepped back a couple of paces.

'I said, step down. Now!' he rasped.

'Marshal Bennett.' The marshal spun around to look at the man coming from the general store who had addressed him. 'I think this gentleman's got a right to be about his business. The name's Wilfred Lacey.' He introduced himself to Ross. 'Chairman of the town council and town lawyer, at your service, sir.'

'I surely hope I won't need your services, Mr Lacey,' Ross said with a wry smile.

'Marshal Bennett,' Lacey intoned.

'He's given me lip, Mr Lacey,' the marshal grated.

'I heard the exchanges between you

and this man. And frankly, I heard nothing that would warrant his detention.'

'I'm wearing the badge, Mr Lacey,' Bennett growled. 'It's my call.'

'And I'm chairman of the town council, and an expert on what constitutes breaking the law, Marshal Bennett,' Wilfred Lacey stated uncompromisingly.

The lawyer was unflinching. 'I believe that you can now be on your way, sir,' he told Caleb Ross.

Ross tipped his hat. 'Obliged, Mr Lacey.'

Caleb Ross rode on, feeling the burn of Bennett's eyes on him.

'Dang it,' he murmured. 'I didn't need another enemy. Particularly one toting a badge!'

10

Sarah Rawl was angry with herself because, try as she might, Caleb Ross kept coming to mind and refused to be shunned. She stubbornly refused to admit to herself that the stranger to the valley had made an impression above and beyond what a brief meeting should have made. Yes, tough he was, but at their meeting at the creek where he had been bathing, she had seen a gentler side to him; a side that had sent her heart skittering the way an impressionable young girl's might, instead of the heart of the older and wiser woman she was.

Her reverie was interrupted by the sound of her brother's hee-hawing as he came along the hall to the den where she was doing the ranch accounts. She did not have long to wait to find out the reason for Scott Rawl's hilarity and mirth. He had no sooner swaggered into the den than he told his sister the reason for his good humour.

'Darnest funny thing, sis,' he guffawed. Jack Sweeney, a man Sarah disliked intensely was with Scott and was even more amused than her brother was. 'The drunks acting as pall bearers at the Watson funeral, because no one else would do the job, dropped the casket.'

Sarah Rawl was rocked by the news.

'It burst open,' Scott leaned on Sweeney, guffawing even more, 'and good old Tom fell right out and landed face down in horse manure!'

'Tom Watson's dead?' Sarah asked, shocked.

'Yeah,' Scott Rawl drawled, as if Watson's death was a matter of fleeting interest. 'Thought he was good enough to draw on Jack.' Rawl sniggered. 'Found out he wasn't near good enough, eh, Jack.'

Fury replacing shock, Sarah Rawl sprang out of her chair. 'A man's death is not a laughing matter, Scott!' she rebuked her brother. Her eyes were hot coals on Sweeney. 'You must have known that Tom Watson was no match for you?'

Sweeney gave a shrug of indifference.

'Wish I'd been there to see it,' Scott Rawl snorted. 'Tom Watson eating horseshit.'

'Get out of the house, Sweeney,' Sarah ordered. 'And don't enter it again.'

'Now hold on a minute,' Scott Rawl railed against his sister. 'Jack's a friend of mine. A good friend, too.'

'He's nothing but a toerag dragging you down to his level,' Sarah Rawl fumed. 'And you can't go any lower than that, Scott.'

She turned her glaring attention on Sweeney.

'You didn't have to kill Tom Watson.'

'He made the play, Miss Rawl,' Jack Sweeney flung back. 'I simply indulged his stupidity.'

'Tom Watson was no gun-slick, and

you knew that, Sweeney. In my book that makes his killing murder.' Sarah Rawl's anger intensified. 'Go one better, Sweeney. Get off Rawl range when you leave the house.'

'I've got pay coming,' he growled.

Sarah Rawl did a quick check on the payroll ledger. She took a roll of dollar bills from the desk drawer, peeled off fifty dollars and threw them across the desk at Sweeney.

'That's more than you've got coming. And,' Sarah's look was one of utter contempt, 'a way more than you're worth.'

Jack Sweeney sneered.

'Heh, Scott, maybe you should wear the petticoat in this outfit, 'cause you sure ain't wearin' the trousers, boy.'

'Don't call me a damn boy, Jack!' Scott Rawl flared.

'Well, you certainly ain't no man,' Sweeney goaded him.

'Jack stays, Sarah,' Rawl barked.

'I don't want scum like him anywhere near me,' Sarah Rawl declared. 'He makes my skin crawl.'

Jack Sweeney shrugged and pocketed his pay.

'Never wanted to work for no damn woman anyway,' he rasped. He turned to leave. 'Of course you could always come with me, Scott,' he said, casually.

Sarah knew that he had cleverly placed a wedge between her and Scott. Scott's pride had been badly dented by her rebuke, and as a result his mood was reckless. She worried that she had over-reacted and had played right into Jack Sweeney's hands.

Scott Rawl was caught between opposing forces. He dithered.

'Unless you feel comfortable in those petticoats, that is,' Sweeney crooned, using the wedge he had engineered to widen further the gap between Scott and his sister.

His ploy proved successful.

'Hell, let's hit the trail, Jack,' Scott Rawl chanted. 'Like you said, a bosslady don't set none too well with me neither.'

Confused as to how to play the hand which Sweeney had so cleverly dealt, Sarah Rawl chose the wrong option.

'You ride out of here with Sweeney and there's no coming back, Scott.'

'That's fine with me, sis. You can have the Rawl ranch, every goddam blade of grass and every stinking cow, too.'

Sarah Rawl knew the deepest depression of the many she had suffered since being forced by her pa to leave her teaching post in town to run the ranch in his absence.

'It'll only be 'til Scott gets enough sense,' Sam Rawl had cajoled, to wear down her resistance. 'A year at most.'

But that had been three years ago, during which time her pa had only paid as many visits to the ranch, always telling her that sooner rather than later, Scott would reach maturity. But she had steadily lost hope that he ever would. Scott Rawl would outwardly age to manhood, but inside Sarah reckoned that he'd always be a brash boy, incapable of the kind of compromise that was needed to live in peace with his neighbours. And the bad influence of Jack Sweeney and others on the Rawl payroll did not help. If she had any sense she would pitch Rawl interests to blazes and return to what she loved — educating the town's youngsters.

Now Scott Rawl was walking out through the door with a toerag. The stock had dwindled due to the constant feuding between Scott and Tom Watson and the neighbouring ranchers, too, and the quality of grass had deteriorated due to Scott's aversion to the hard work of diverting water from creeks and streams to irrigate the range as the boundaries of the ranch had been extended. A right mess she'd be presenting to her pa when he arrived on his next visit from Washington. In fact, if the downward spiral continued for much longer, there would be no Rawl ranch for Sam Rawl to come home to.

'Wait,' Sarah said.

Scott Rawl turned round instantly,

which Sarah took as a sign of his reluctance really to leave. On the other hand, Jack Sweeney turned slowly, smiling triumphantly, knowing that he had Sarah over a barrel.

'Maybe if you spent a while repairing line shacks that need fixing, Sweeney,' she suggested, as a way out of the impasse.

Jack Sweeney took a long time to answer. When he did, Sarah knew how much over a barrel he really had her.

'Hard work, fixing up line shacks, Miss Rawl,' he said, brazenly dismissing her suggestion.

Curling up inside, Sarah offered the no-good Jack Sweeney the pay rise that she reckoned was his condition for letting her off the hook she was dangling on; a pay rise on top of the pay he already had and of which he had not earned a dime.

'Ten dollars a month increase in pay, OK?' she asked.

'That's a good offer, Jack,' Scott Rawl said hopefully.

'Mighty generous, ma'am,' Sweeney purred, clever enough not to refuse her offer and lose Scott Rawl's backing.

'You'll stay, Jack?' Scott Rawl asked eagerly.

'Winter's not far off. So I guess if I'm moving on, spring will be a lot more pleasant to do it in.'

'I'm sure glad that all that's settled,' Scott enthused.

But Sarah Rawl knew that far from it being ended, it was only beginning. But her concession to Sweeney would give her time to try and talk sense to her brother. However, it would be an uphill battle for her to persuade him that Jack Sweeney was a bottom-of-the-bucket no-good.

* * *

Caleb Ross had not missed the man who had sneaked out of town after him. But his lack of knowledge about the territory's geography had him at a disadvantage, and a short time ago he had lost sight of his tracker, for Ross was certain that that was what the man was — probably a Rawl hand, paid to hang around town to report any goings on that might have the potential to harm Rawl interests. And he had plenty to report back with now. He had probably ridden ahead, but then again, he might not have.

Though the valley in which the Rawl ranch was situated offered little by way of bushwhack country, the terrain between town and the valley (like the country he was riding through right now) had creeks, gullies, draws and canyons, where an entire army could hide and not be seen until it was way too late to do anything about it. One such canyon was just up ahead. He could skirt it, but the surrounding terrain did not offer any obvious advantage.

So he rode on into the canyon.

★   ★   ★

Jack Sweeney left the Rawl ranch house with a swagger that made Sarah Rawl sick to the stomach. And seeing Scott in his poisonous company depressed her no end. That she had tried her best since her pa had taken off to Washington and left her with the responsibility for the running of the ranch, was no consolation to her now. At first Scott had groused a lot, but he had come round and thrown in his lot with Sarah. The men had not liked the idea of taking orders from a woman, but Scott had persuaded them that Sarah's tenure would be short and that Sam Rawl would soon tire of Washington and return to what he knew and loved best — raising cows. Or alternatively, that should his pa run for political office, then he'd take over the running of the ranch. On Scott's assurance that Sarah was only a caretaker rather than a long-term boss, the men rowed in behind her. However, as Sam Rawl's stay in Washington lengthened and he insisted on Sarah remaining on as boss of the ranch the men grew uneasy, as had Scott. Becoming increasingly disgruntled, Scott Rawl withdrew his goodwill from Sarah, and had in fact actively begun to foster discontent and rebellion among the men in the hope that Sam Rawl would yield to his demands that he should take over from Sarah. This was Sarah Rawl's wish also. But her pa being as stubborn as his son, neither man would give way, and Sarah had to watch as the ranch deteriorated and discipline vanished. Until now, Sarah, had had to fight tooth and nail for every order to be obeyed, and had to suffer the humiliation of having her orders first checked out with Scott. Only the previous month she had sent an urgent wire to her pa seeking his immediate return. As previously, he had promised that he would come, but he had not. She could not understand why a man would spend the best part of his life building something, only then to throw it all away on a crazy whim. It made no sense at all to the practically minded Sarah Rawl.

'God, how I wish I could just go back to being a teacher,' she wailed, as Jack Sweeney threw an arm round Scott Rawl's shoulder and sneered back at the house from where Sarah was watching through the parlour window.

Whatever he whispered in Scott's ear brought a loud and vulgar guffaw from him. They went and joined a group of men lounging at the corral, and moments later Scott's guffaw was taken up by the men as Jack Sweeney, acting out the story, relayed the unfortunate and gruesome happening in town.

Angered, Sarah stormed to the front door and threw it open.

'Don't you men have anything to do but lounge around the place?' she barked. 'You could start with mending the fences you're leaning on!'

'Kinda hot right now, ma'am,' Jack Sweeney piped up, taking on the role of spokesman.

'I'm not paying you men to idle!' Sarah snapped. She glared at a sneering

Sweeney. 'That goes for you too, Sweeney.'

'Ease up, sis,' Scott Rawl said, stepping forward. 'I'll talk to the men.' He turned to the lounging men. 'Sarah is right. Start with the corral fence!'

Surprised by Scott Rawl's stern rebuke, the men looked at each other uncertainly, and then to Jack Sweeney for direction.

'You heard what Mr Rawl said, you lazy layabouts!' Sweeney bellowed.

While the men put their backs into repairing the corral fence, Scott and Jack Sweeney rode off. Sarah was of a mind to remind Sweeney that he had no special privileges, but held back because of the aggravation it might cause. As she shut the front door, she hated herself for her lack of courage. Slowly but surely Jack Sweeney was worming his way into Rawl business, until soon, to all intents and purposes, if she was not careful, Sweeney would effectively be the boss of the ranch.

'God damn it, Pa!' she swore

vehemently. 'Get back here right now, if you don't want to be working for Jack Sweeney when you do!'

★ ★ ★

The sound of his horse's hoofs on the shale track were loud in the uncommon silence of the canyon. Caleb Ross drew rein to listen, searching the stillness for any hint of trouble. He heard none, but that did not mean that it wasn't there. In fact, in his experience, the kind of breathless silence that pervaded the canyon was often the precursor of trouble.

Ross let his eyes drift along the high reaches of the canyon, where a lone vulture circled above the sun-scorched heights. Vultures were canny critters. Was this one anticipating a meal? Was the vulture, from his lofty perch, seeing what he could not see from the floor of the canyon?

When a second and third vulture joined the first, Caleb Ross was sure

123

that he had company; company that had no interest in announcing its presence. Therefore, it had to be assumed that the reason for the watcher's silence was malign intent and not shyness. He could turn back, but the bushwhacker might be behind him. So he might as well ride on. This Caleb Ross did, hoping for a glint of sun on a rifle barrel; a puff of dust as a man shifted position. Or the sound of a pebble dislodged by a boot, to warn him.

*　*　*

Stretch Crowther was the name of the man waiting for Ross to come close enough for him to be reasonably sure of hitting him with his first bullet. Miss, and Ross would be on him in no time at all. At the very least he would have to wound him badly enough for him to be able to make his way down into the canyon to finish him off. He was not an ace shot. In fact he seldom had use for

124

a gun. His service to Scott Rawl was to hang around town and keep his eyes and ears open, and to report back to Rawl on any possible trouble brewing. Of late, folk had begun to tire of Scott Rawl's antics, and his close association with Jack Sweeney had pretty much been the final nail in the young rancher's coffin, because Sweeney was pure poison; the kind of dregs that no half-decent town would want around. And now, as the stranger called Caleb Ross, who had had the audacity to buck Scott Rawl, came into his rifle sights, he regretted not having done as he was supposed to do and just ridden on to the ranch to inform Scott Rawl about Ross's thorny brush with Dan Bennett, the marshal of Ghost Creek, and Scott Rawl's protector and enforcer. And it wasn't really the confrontation between Bennett and Ross that mattered, interesting though it was. What was really interesting was the way Wilfred Lacey, the town lawyer and town council chairman, had reined in Dan

Bennett. And the reaction of the onlookers, who had given their silent backing to Lacey's rebuke of the marshal.

Caleb Ross was a wild spark in dry scrub. And all it would take for a full-blown inferno would be for the wind to blow that spark in the right direction. The good folk of Ghost Creek might be seeing in Ross the man who would finally tame Scott Rawl and his cronies, particularly Jack Sweeney. That was what would interest Scott Rawl no end.

However, as he tracked Ross out of town, Stretch Crowther had begun to think about handing Rawl the solution rather than the problem, by killing Caleb Ross. Crowther was fed up with being the dogsbody hand in the Rawl outfit, and longed to get higher on the ladder than the lowest rung. But what had seemed like a crackerjack idea when he had first thought about it, had lost most of its sparkle now that Caleb Ross was almost upon him. His hands shook. He had never actually killed a man in cold blood before, and now that he was about to, Stretch Crowther could not decide whether he liked the power he held over Ross's life, or regretted the downward track he had chosen. Once he pulled the trigger of the Winchester, he could never again be the man he had been. He'd be someone else — a cold-blooded killer. And he could not be sure whether he could live with that other man, until that man emerged out of the darkness of his deed.

Caleb Ross came into Stretch Crowther's rifle sights.

11

Marshal Dan Bennett was skulking in his office in Ghost Creek. He was not an intelligent man, but he was a cunning *hombre*, and he knew that his hold over the town, which he had enjoyed ever since Scott Rawl had forced the town council (by threatening to withdraw Rawl business from the town's traders, most of whom sat on the council) to make him the marshal above more honourable candidates, was tenuous.

Dan Bennett's past was littered with indiscretions of one kind or another. He had spent time with an outlaw gang. Had run guns. And had on occasion hired out his gun to men like Scott Rawl. However, no solid proof of his misdeeds could be offered to the town council meeting that had made him marshal, and Wilfred Lacey, much to his later regret when Dan Bennett's spots began to show, had argued that rumour and hearsay were not evidence. He had asked Bennett at the time if there was any truth in the stories about his past, confident that his skill and experience as an advocate would help him to see through any shilly-shallying on Bennett's part. But Dan Bennett was much too skilled and accomplished a liar, and when he denied his past he did so with the ring of truth. However, he was not shy about his past when it suited his needs, and as a reference for Scott Rawl's purposes, his past could not be more appropriate. Rawl had, with the prompting of Jack Sweeney, whom Bennett had known from their stay in an outlaw roost, put Bennett in his pay to tighten his grip on the town and its hinterland, and Bennett had served him well, not hestitating to bust heads when Rawl intentions were questioned. He'd have gone further too, only Rawl was content, at least for the time being, with only strong-arm tactics. It would take time for Jack Sweeney to completely poison the young rancher's mind, but he was making swift progress. When that had been achieved and he controlled Rawl's every move, Sweeney had plans to have Sarah Rawl meet with an accident. With her out of the way, Jack Sweeney would hold total sway over the Rawl ranch and its coffers; coffers he intended plundering as quickly as he could manage.

'I'll see you right when the big payout comes, Dan,' he had promised Bennett. 'Added to what you're pocketing right now, it should make the years ahead nice and cosy.' He'd chuckled.

The second part of his plan, with the crooked marshal's help, was to plunder the town itself. To do that he intended, in time, to make Ghost Creek an open town where the dregs of the West would be made welcome, at a price of course.

But now there was an unexpected fly in the ointment by the name of Caleb Ross.

'Ross needs to be dealt with, Dan,'

Sweeney had said on a visit to the law office the previous night, after he had gunned down Tom Watson in cold blood. 'When he comes into town, I'm sure you'll find a way to make sure that he stays put.' He'd laughed harshly. 'In a nice pine box, of course.'

On the street an hour ago he had tried to rile the stranger called Ross. Had he succeeded in doing so, it would have been easy to shoot Ross in the back, and use the hoary old story that Ross had tried to bust out of jail. But he had learned that Caleb Ross was not an easy man to rile. And Wilfred Lacey's intervention had, to say the least, been untimely and unexpected. In fact Lacey's intervention worried him greatly. The shift in the town's mood was barely noticeable yet. But, like a hairline crack in a china teacup, there was no knowing when the crack would widen and the cup would fragment. The cup could last for years, or its fragmentation might just be seconds away. It was a suitable analogy to draw with the town's mood since Caleb Ross had spurned his challenge. He had seen towns turn before, and often all it took was for a man of the calibre of Ross to step forward for other men to draw strength from him. Ross had clearly got Wilfred Lacey in his camp already. How many more would join him? That was Dan Bennett's dilemma. Should he continue to hang around and hope that the backbone Caleb Ross had put into the town would be just a brief flirtation with bravery? Or should he gather his illgotten gains and hit the trail while he still had the chance? It would be a pity to have to throw away a future share in Jack Sweeney's plans. But, he reasoned sensibly, full pockets were of no use to a dead man.

Of course the town traders, and those who depended on Rawl's largesse, would be slow to act against him. But they just might risk going against Scott Rawl if they figured that Sarah Rawl would become the boss of the Rawl ranch in fact rather than name. She had a loyalty to the people of the valley and Ghost Creek that her brother had not, and she would not do as Scott Rawl had threatened, and that was to have the ranch supplies freighted in from Danesville, a town about fifteen miles north of Ghost Creek. Sarah Rawl understood the value of neighbourly relations and a sound economy that would benefit all. But were Scott Rawl to be removed from the scene his sister would have no truck with him, and that would mean the end of a very lucrative income.

Dan Bennett was facing a sizeable crux. He knew that soon he would have to jump. But which way, that was his problem and his worry. However, there was one ray of hope that Bennett clung to, albeit a slim one. He had seen Stretch Crowther ride out of town on Caleb Ross's tail, probably to report to Scott Rawl. But Bennett was a shrewd reader of men, and he had seen a purpose in Crowther which he had not seen before: the kind of purpose a man who was tussling with a problem gets. He was aware of Crowther's saloon grousing about being the butt end of the Rawl outfit, and now his hope was that Crowther would see in Caleb Ross's demise the road to Scott Rawl's favour and a more prestigious standing in Rawl affairs. But if Stretch Crowther was thinking along those lines, would his resolve and purpose hold long enough to get the job done?

Dan Bennett could only wish that it would.

★ ★ ★

Furious with her brother's sucking up to trash like Jack Sweeney, Sarah Rawl did as she had done since she was a young girl to rid herself of her frustration, and that was to ride like the wind out across the range to the hills and canyons beyond, until she was fit to fall out of the saddle as her fury drained away and left her limp.

Her frustration was all the keener

because she felt so helpless to get to grips with the running of the ranch. She had always known that, being a woman, she'd need Scott's help and co-operation to fulfil the role into which her pa had pitched her, unfairly in her opinion.

'Of course at first you'll find that bossing the ranch will be tough going, you being a woman,' Sam Rawl had openly conceded, when she had questioned the wisdom of his decision. 'But you're a Rawl woman. Tough as nails and rattler-mean when needs be. Just like your ma was, rest her soul.'

He'd laughed in remembrance.

'Your ma would have taken a whip to any man who'd question her orders or give her guff.'

His laughter deepened.

'It got so that the men would rather take my boot in their backside than tussle with your ma, Sarah.'

'Scott won't like it any,' she had warned her father.

'I'll talk to Scott. He'll understand,'

he'd reassured her. 'In a couple of years, when he's shed the green still in him, he'll be ready to boss the ranch. Then you can go back to what you love best — teaching.'

Sam Rawl knew his son well, and at first it had been as he had said it would be, until the day Jack Sweeney happened by, just on the very day that their foreman had quit. From the start, Sarah had been against hiring Sweeney, but she could not give Scott a good reason why Sweeney would not fit in, and he had put her reservations about Jack Sweeney's suitability down to what he called her *woman's vagaries*.

'Let Sweeney show us if he can do what he claims he can do, sis,' Scott Rawl had offered by way of compromise.

Sarah had foolishly agreed. In a couple of days she would talk to Scott again and change his mind. The woolly-headedness of her thinking soon became very clear, even by the end of that day of which there had only been half left when Sweeney had ridden in. She recalled looking out the window of the den and seeing Scott and Jack Sweeney joking and laughing like age-old *compadres*, and she had immediately known that there would be no persuading Scott to relent on Jack Sweeney's long-term hiring now.

'Darn it, sis,' Scott had argued with her, 'Jack'll be an ace ramrod. Knows more about cows than I'll ever learn in two lifetimes.'

'But I don't think Sweeney will fit in here, Scott,' Sarah had desperately opined.

'Another one of your woman's vagaries, huh,' Scott Rawl had groaned. 'Anyway, it ain't no good us arguing about it,' he'd said. 'I've already told Jack that he's got a Rawl job for as long as he wants it.'

Sarah had been shocked. Up until then most of the decisions had been taken in co-operation with Scott. But when agreement could not be reached, she had had the final say.

'You had no right to hire Sweeney

without asking me, Scott,' she had berated him.

'It's about time I got equal say round here, Sarah,' Scott had said, defiantly truculent. 'Pa's been gone a year now, and I figure that I've shed the green he talked about.' He pulled himself up to his full height. 'I figure it's about time you got back to teaching, sis, and left Rawl ranch business to me.'

Sarah now understood Jack Sweeney's huddle with Scott before he had entered the house.

'That'll be for Pa to decide, Scott,' she'd said, with as much authority as she could muster.

Scott had laughed in a way she had not heard him laugh before, crudely and harshly. 'Best get it into your head, Sarah. Pa's got politico sickness, bad at that. I figure cows don't interest him no more. And that means that the Rawl ranch needs the kind of looking after that a woman can't give it.'

'I'm still boss round here, Scott,' Sarah had railed defiantly.

'Well now,' Scott drawled. 'I don't see it that way no more, sis.'

'You mean Jack Sweeney doesn't see it that way any more, isn't that so, Scott?' she had responded hotly.

Scott had stormed out of the house and right into Jack Sweeney's honeypot. Sarah knew that she had reacted wrongly, and had played into Jack Sweeney's hands. In the intervening months it had come as no surprise that Rawl relations with their neighbours and the citizens of Ghost Creek had become increasingly fraught, as Jack Sweeney wove his evil web ever more tightly round Scott. So desperate had her situation become, as she watched Scott change from a hard-working, pleasant and easy-going fella to a brawling trouble-maker, that Sarah Rawl had even thought about killing Sweeney herself, or having him killed. However, she could not bring herself to do or commission an act of cold-blooded murder. She had no doubt that what was her weakness was Jack

Sweeney's strength, and all she could hope for was that Scott would one day soon see through Sweeney's charade of comradeship into his rotten core. But there weren't that many days left for that to happen. In a short time there would be nothing left for her and Scott to wrangle about. The Rawl ranch, once the finest ranch in the valley, was fast sliding into decay. Most days Sweeney and Scott lounged around town, if there was no one in the valley they could pick a fight with. And more and more the ranch hands were taking their pay without giving a return. Or on the odd occasion when Scott listened to her and ordered the men to work, they turned in slipshod work that was often more harmful than productive.

Riding at a full gallop towards the hills and canyons where she knew she would find the excitement of riding the rims relaxing, Sarah Rawl came to a decision. She would set out for Washington and drag her pa back, by the scruff of the neck if necessary!

From under the brim of his hat, Caleb Ross watched the circling vultures, five of the critters now, which left no doubt that they saw a meal in the offing. He watched as the ugly flesh-eaters tightened the circle, jostling for position, wanting to be first to feast. He was not an expert on the behaviour of vultures, but he reckoned that he could trust in their greed, and when they dropped lower and lower still as he drew nearer to a ledge that bulged out from the rockface just ahead like a fat man's belly, he figured that he was close to the bushwhacker's lair. The ambusher had chosen well. Even if Ross got a chance, it would be nigh impossible to dislodge the shooter.

There was a shale track at either side of the ledge. The right-sided track ended short of the ledge in a tumble of boulders which might offer cover in which to wait for the bushwhacker to make a mistake. The short, open stretch of ground immediately beyond the boulders would make waiting necessary, as any attempt to bridge it, so close to the ledge, would most likely prove fatal. All the ambusher would have to do was wait as well. There was the cover of the overhanging rockface at the top of the canyon above him to protect him from the blazing sun, whereas the man in the boulders would fry in its blistering heat.

The hostile terrain had already chosen the winner of such a stand-off.

The left-sided track was steeper, and had more shale to lose purchase on. And at the top, the track twisted at an angle that gave very little scope for a clear shot at the ambusher. Overall, he was faced with a problem, the solution of which presently evaded him.

Caleb Ross cast his eyes upwards.

'If there's any luck left in that pot I've been dipping into of late, Lord,' he murmured, 'I'd sure appreciate your co-operation in letting me dip one more time.'

★ ★ ★

The heat rising up from the floor of the canyon made Caleb Ross shimmer in the Winchester's sights. Stretch Crowther's finger applied pressure to the rifle's trigger. He tried to swallow but his mouth was as dry as the sandy floor of the canyon. Beads of perspiration rolled off his forehead. He wiped them away before they stung his eyes. He forced himself to wait until Ross came out of the shimmer and clearly into view.

The seconds dragged. Crowther's breathing became more and more shallow as his lungs constricted. A dull ache began behind his eyes, and spread out across the top of his head in a throbbing crown that tightened, vice-like, with each heartbeat.

Then Caleb Ross became clear in his rifle sights, and Stretch Crowther triggered the Winchester.

12

The appearance of a rider on top of the canyon galloping hell for leather along its rim, seemingly unheeding of the danger, took Stretch Crowther by surprise and he took his eye off his target for a split second just as the Winchester bucked. Trapped by the steep walls of the canyon, the crack of the rifle bounced and echoed along its length, the rockfaces continuously reshaping the sound as it progressed. On hearing the crack of the Winchester, the rider on the rim drew rein. Meanwhile Caleb Ross's hat spun in the air as Crowther's bullet snatched it from his head. He wasted no time in throwing himself from the saddle into a shallow dip in the ground, which offered some cover but not enough. As bad luck would have it, he was in a particularly bald stretch of the canyon.

Sarah Rawl stood in her stirrups to look down into the canyon from where she figured the shot had come, and saw a crouched man scrambling along a ledge.

'Right below me,' she called out to Caleb Ross.

The scurrying figure looked familiar, and when he looked up Sarah Rawl drew a sharp breath on recognizing a Rawl hand. She could not put a name to the man, but she did know that his importance to the running of Rawl affairs was negligible.

'Stay right where you are,' she ordered Crowther.

Stretch Crowther might have listened, if Caleb Ross's bullet had not buzzed off the rockface inches from his face. Panic flared in Crowther's eyes and he scrambled up the continuation of the left-sided shale track to the brush-covered plateau above, where he had hitched his horse. However, running on shale was slow and precarious progress. Stretch Crowther slid back two paces for each one forward, and his panic became all the greater as Ross stung his right shoulder with a bullet. It was only a graze, but it was enough with Crowther's bleary-eyed anxiety to throw him off balance: a balance he scrambled to regain but failed. He spun out of control, his hands clutching at anything and everything, but his clawing fingers found no purchase. He staggered backwards on to the ledge, his legs doing a crazy dance as his momentum took him to the edge and over. Stretch Crowther's ear-splitting scream as he plunged headlong down into the canyon filled every inch of space. Caleb Ross retched on hearing Crowther's bone-crushing collision with the rocky floor of the canyon.

The silence that followed was even louder than Stretch Crowther's scream.

Sarah Rawl swayed in the saddle and Ross held his breath, fearing that were she to pass out she would follow Crowther. It was with immense relief that he saw her steady herself and recover.

'Thank you, Miss Rawl,' he called out.

'I don't want your thanks, Mr Ross,' she shouted back. 'What I do want is your departure from this valley. It seems that the Grim Reaper rides with you, sir.'

'He'd have killed me,' Ross said unsympathetically. 'So don't expect me to feel sorry.'

'I don't expect anything at all from you, Mr Ross,' Sarah Rawl said.

She vanished from the rim of the canyon.

'Be seeing you in a little while, ma'am,' he murmured.

* * *

Marshal Dan Bennett heard the rush of feet to the law office door, and knew instinctively before the door was flung open what was about to happen. Wilfred Lacey, the town Lawyer and chairman of the town council was leading a delegation of councillors and prominent citizens.

'Marshal Bennett, I'll come straight to the point,' Lacey began. 'After an emergency meeting, the town council has unanimously decided that your fitness for office does not meet the high standards that wearing a marshal's badge requires. Consequently, you're fired!' he stated bluntly.

Bennett thought about challenging the council's vote, until he saw the ever deepening crowd gathering outside in the street. It seemed he didn't have a friend or a backer left in Ghost Creek.

'If you take my badge, who else is going to pin it on,' he growled. 'With more and more trouble brewing by the day, I reckon the answer is no one will.'

'We've already got a man in mind, Bennett,' Wilfred Lacey said.

'Yeah,' he said, surprised. 'Who?'

'The man who stood up to you today. This town is sick of you running it to suit Scott Rawl and his no-good sidekick Jack Sweeney, Bennett.'

'If you take my badge, Scott won't like it any,' Bennett warned. 'He'll shift his business to Danesville, like he threatened he would.'

It pleased Bennett to see the uneasy shifting of the traders in the council delegation and the crowd outside with a stake to protect.

'Ya know,' Bennett sat back into his chair, smug and cocky, 'I think I'll keep this badge for just a spell longer, Lacey,' he said, confident that he had the majority of the town council on the run.

When Lacey leaned across the desk and ripped the marshal's badge from his shirt, taking most of the shirt-front with it, Dan Bennett wasn't the only surprised man around. Lacey threw a roll of dollar bills on the marshal's desk.

'That's the month's pay due,' he said. 'Now get out!'

Bennett studied the faces of the delegation for a sign of dissent which he could exploit, but all eyes slid away from his. Now that Wilfred Lacey had taken the initiative, no man wanted to be the one to throw Bennett a lifeline. Another consideration was that if they lost Rawl business they would badly need town business, and any trader who opposed Lacey, one of Ghost Creek's most prominent citizens, might be punished where it mattered, at the cash till. The majority of the citizens of Ghost Creek had suffered Scott Rawl and his cohorts for long enough, their antics backed or ignored by Dan Bennett. And now that there was a chance that they could be freed of Rawl rowdyism and Bennett connivance, they'd not thank anyone who jeopardized that opportunity.

'Time to be moving along, Bennett,' Lacey said.

Dan Bennett struck a defiant pose.

'Scott Rawl won't stand for this,' he warned, raising his voice to be heard on the street. Not for one darn second, I reckon.'

Then he issued a second, chilling warning:

'Neither will Jack Sweeney. Who happens to be a personal friend of mine.'

The mention of Sweeney, even in passing, shook the resolute Wilfred Lacey.

'Still want my badge, Lacey?' he sneered.

All eyes were on the town lawyer. Bennett took pleasure and comfort in the bob of Lacey's Adam's apple. However, his surprise was utter when the lawyer pinned on the marshal's badge.

'If the council is agreeable, I'll act as the town marshal until a suitable replacement can be found.'

Stunned by this unexpected twist, the council members nodded their heads in agreement. One member did find his voice to sound a note of caution.

'You're not gun-handy, Wilfred,' he said. 'At least not gun-handy enough to be a marshal.'

'I'll only hold office until I can persuade Mr Ross to take over. I'll seek him out tomorrow.'

'And if he don't want the job?' Bennett queried.

'Then I guess my tenure will be a little longer, Bennett,' was Wilfred Lacey's gutsy reply.

Dan Bennett strolled to the law office door. 'Dangerous job, being a marshal,' he said.

'Is that a threat?' Lacey barked.

'All I'm doing is giving you kindly advice, Marshal Lacey,' Bennett snorted.

The former marshal of Ghost Creek pushed his way through the crowd clustered round the law office door.

'You can't be serious about toting a badge, Wilfred?' the council member who had spoken up questioned the town lawyer. 'And that was no kindly word of advice Bennett gave you.'

'I'm ready right now to hand over this badge to any man who'll wear it, Ned,' Lacey said. No one stepped forward. 'Look, the thing is, it's about time that this town stood against the likes of Bennett and Rawl and Sweeney, and Rawl's evergrowing band of hard-cases.'

'Are you willing to die to see the back of them?' a second council member asked the lawyer.

'No. I'm damn well not,' Lacey stated fierily. 'But neither am I willing to go on living in a town where every blink of my eyes needs Scott Rawl and Jack Sweeney's approval!'

The lawyer went and sat behind the marshal's desk.

'Now you folks go home.' He looked at the paper-strewn desk. 'Looks like Bennett didn't care much for paper-work, so I've got a lot to do.'

The crowd drifted away, giving Wilfred Lacey the chance to shake in his boots in private. 'You must be the dumbest bastard I know,' he groaned.

★ ★ ★

Still smarting from her run-in with Caleb Ross, Sarah Rawl charged into the ranch yard at breakneck speed, forcing a group of men who were joshing and joking with Jack Sweeney and her brother to leap aside.

'What the hell do you think you're doing, Sarah,' Scott roared after her. 'You damn near ran us down, woman.'

Sarah ignored his angry rebuke and went inside the house.

'Looks like Miss Rawl don't much care 'bout giving you an answer, Scott,' Jack Sweeney snorted.

'I'll get a damn answer!' Rawl growled. He strode off to the house, headed for the den. He threw open the door. 'When I ask a question, Sarah, I expect an answer, you hear!'

'Get a couple of men saddled up,' she said. 'There's a body to be collected in Gulch Canyon.'

Scott Rawl stopped mid-stride. 'A body, you say. Whose body?'

'I don't know his name.'

'Well, we ain't no funeral service, sis.'

'He's a Rawl hand. Lanky, a nose like a jutting rock.'

'That sounds like Stretch Crowther.' Scott Rawl's lips narrowed. 'How did he get killed?'

'He tried to bushwhack Caleb Ross, but he didn't kill him. Crowther fell off a ledge when Ross winged him.'

'Then in my book he killed him,' Rawl stated grimly.

'Stretch Crowther earned the trouble he got, Scott. Just go and fetch his body back to the ranch for burial.'

'What was he doing in Gulch Canyon anyway?' Rawl wondered. 'Crowther's job was to hang around town and keep his ears and eyes open.'

'Maybe he followed Ross from town,' Sarah speculated. 'And maybe he thought he could do you a favour by killing him, Scott.'

Sarah Rawl ran agitated fingers through her thick coal-black hair.

'When is all this trouble going to stop, Scott?'

'When this valley from one end to the

other is Rawl range,' Scott Rawl said. 'That's when the trouble will stop.'

'I'm going to see Pa in Washington,' Sarah declared.

'Now why would you want to do that, sis?'

'To ask him to come home, before it's too late.'

'There's no need to worry Pa,' he growled menacingly.

'There's every need, Scott,' Sarah said, unfazed. 'Before the Rawl ranch is nothing more than skinny cows, dusty earth due to lack of irrigation, and dry water-holes.'

'I've been busy protecting Rawl boundaries,' Rawl chanted.

'I want to see the back of Jack Sweeney, Scott,' she declared.

'Jack goes or stays on my say-so,' Scott flung back angrily.

'I boss this ranch, Scott. And I say he goes. Now!'

'You're a skirt, Sarah. Skirts don't boss ranches.' He spun round. 'Now I guess I'd best go get old Stretch back to the ranch for burial before the vultures gobble up every speck of him. Then, after Stretch has had earth shovelled in his face, I reckon Jack Sweeney and me had better pay Ross a visit.'

He sneered. 'Tell him how much better off he'd be if he just upped and left.'

'Stay away from Caleb Ross, Scott,' Sarah Rawl pleaded. 'He's a cut above what you and Sweeney have gotten used to.'

'I'm not sure I like you holding Ross in such regard, sis,' he drawled. 'You're a Rawl. You just remember that.'

Scott Rawl stormed out of the den. Almost immediately Sarah Rawl had a new worry added to the pile that was already overwhelming her.

'That new feller Ross is ridin' in, Mr Rawl,' a man shouted.

13

Caleb Ross saw the rush of men to the Rawl yard from every corner, necks craning, faces alive with curiosity and expectancy. He saw Sarah Rawl come from the house to look out from the porch, anxiety in her movements. And Ross himself was not free of anxiety. He was riding into the lion's den, an act of numskull bravado, as most other men would see it. But he was driven by the need to bring to justice the man who had gunned down Tom Watson, and the man who had humiliated him by branding him like a steer. It was that humiliation which had driven Tom to seek the solace of liquor in the Ghost Creek saloon, which caused his death. By now he could count at least twenty men and twenty guns. But his count was one of spec, because the crowd was continuously moving, men changing places to get a better view of the excitement they were expecting Caleb Ross's visit to arouse. As he drew near, Scott Rawl stepped forward to the front of the crowd in the company of the snake-eyed Jack Sweeney.

'Don't recall issuing you with an invite, mister,' Scott Rawl barked, as Ross rode into the yard. 'In fact you're trespassing. And that, 'round here, is a hanging offence.'

'You know, Rawl,' Caleb Ross drawled, 'you've got a mighty big mouth when you've got a small army to back you. Are you so lippy, man to man?'

Sarah Rawl tensed.

Goaded, Scott Rawl's hand dropped to his sixgun. Jack Sweeney grabbed Rawl's wrist to stay his hand, but only on seeing Ross's hand move faster.

'I can take him any time I want!' Scott Rawl yelled, shoving Sweeney aside.

'Sure you can, Scott,' Sweeney said diplomatically.

'No, he can't,' Ross said. 'And you're headed for a rope, Sweeney.'

'Yeah. What for?' Jack Sweeney sneered.

'Murder,' Ross stated.

'Murder, huh?' Sweeney chuckled. 'But I didn't murder no one, mister.'

'You murdered Tom Watson,' Ross said.

Jack Sweeney shook his head. 'Watson was skunk-drunk and bucking for trouble. And *he* called me out. That's not murder, Ross. That's called self-defence.'

'As you said, Tom Watson was skunk-drunk, and he wasn't gun-slick. In fact Tom wore a gun for fashion, not for shooting with.'

'That's sure a dangerous and dumb thing to do,' Sweeney said.

'And you knew that, Sweeney,' Caleb Ross stated. 'And when you drew on Tom Watson, you knew that he didn't stand anywhere near an equal chance. That makes killing Tom murder. And when the facts are put before a judge and jury, you'll hang for sure, I reckon.'

Jack Sweeney laughed. When his laughter trailed off, he changed his stance and his eyes became glistening black pebbles.

'I aim to keep my neck exactly the same length it is right now, Ross.' His hands hovered over the two-gun rig, slung low on his hips.

Now it was Scott Rawl's turn to act as peacemaker. He spoke in a whisper to Jack Sweeney, and as he did, the hardcase's grin widened.

'Ya know, Ross,' Sweeney said, when the whispering was over, 'I don't want to mess up the yard and scare Miss Rawl. I don't have any worries 'bout going to jail.'

A stir of amazement rippled through the assembled men at the unexpectedness of Sweeney's capitulation.

'Marshal Bennett saw what happened in the saloon. Saw Watson draw first. Once he tells a jury that, I'll walk free.'

Caleb Ross snorted.

'I don't know much about Bennett,' he said. 'But I figure he's a cat's paw in Rawl pay.'

'Well now, that might be your view, Ross,' Scott Rawl said. 'But then your opinion around here ain't worth a jug of cow piss!'

'Saddle me a nag,' Sweeney ordered one of the hands.

Jack Sweeney unbuckled his guns and tossed them to Ross. The assembled hands were even more amazed. And Caleb Ross was the most surprised man of all.

'Let's burn trail,' the hardcase said, vaulting into the saddle of the mare upon which the man had slung a saddle.

'My business here ain't finished,' Ross declared.

Sarah Rawl's delight at seeing the back of Jack Sweeney, if only for a brief spell in which she hoped to be able to persuade Scott to dump him as a worker and a pal, vanished on hearing Caleb Ross's steely statement.

'Not finished, you say?' Scott Rawl challenged.

'No,' Caleb Ross said grimly. 'I also want the man who put the Rawl brand on Tom Watson.'

'No man would brand another man with a branding-iron,' Sarah Rawl intervened. 'That would be more cruel than killing Tom Watson.'

'I figure that it was the humiliation of being branded like a cow that finally got him killed, ma'am,' Ross said. 'Tom Watson was a proud man. He'd find living with the Rawl brand on his back too hard.'

'Any man would,' Sarah Rawl readily conceded. 'But I think you must be mistaken when you say — '

'No mistake!' Ross interjected. 'I saw it.' Caleb Ross's gaze settled on the man who, at the confrontation with Rawl at the creek, had mentioned branding a man who had been found trespassing on Rawl range. 'You,' he growled. 'Tell us again about the man who was branded for trespassing on Rawl grass.'

The man shifted uneasily under Caleb Ross's burning gaze, and Sarah Rawl's shocked stare.

'Don't know what you're t-talkin' 'b-bout, mister,' the man stammered.

Ross's gun flashed from leather.

'Talk or die,' he barked.

A clear line immediately opened up in front of the man as the other hands got out of the line of fire.

'Talk, Reilly,' Sarah Rawl demanded. 'Is what Mr Ross says true?'

The man called Reilly exchanged a swift and worried glance with Scott Rawl. Caleb Ross thumbed back the hammer of his .45. Perspiration as thick as honey coated Reilly's face, and his eyes filled with a terrible fear.

'It was Mr Rawl did the brandin'!' he whined.

'Clear out before I kill you, Reilly,' Scott Rawl roared.

'Sure, Mr Rawl,' Reilly whined, on an even more pitiful note, and began a fumbling run, hurried on his way by bullets from Scott Rawl's sixgun.

'Scott?' Sarah Rawl said in disbelief.

'It just started out as fun,' Rawl said. 'But Watson wouldn't shut his mouth, sis. I told him. I said, shut your mouth or I'll brand you. He said that I wasn't man enough. So I had to do it, Sarah. You understand, don't you?'

Sarah Rawl backed away as Scott approached her. And then turned and ran weeping to the house. Scott Rawl spun round.

'I'm going to kill you, Ross,' he vowed.

14

'Not with an empty gun, you're not,' Ross retorted. 'You've emptied the chamber putting legs under Reilly.'

'Yeah,' Rawl bellowed insanely. He pulled the trigger of the pistol again and again, each time getting the hollow sound of an empty chamber. 'Someone give me a gun!' he yelled.

But by now, fearful of the revenge Ross must take on Scott Rawl, the gathered men had fallen well out of Rawl's reach. Caleb Ross landed a hammer-hard fist on Rawl's jaw. He went down heavily, and didn't move. Gunless, Jack Sweeney looked on, unable to intervene. Ross beckoned to the nearest man.

'Get him up,' he ordered. And when the man had done so, he delivered another order: 'Now get a bucket of water and throw it on him.' That done, he had one more order: 'Get him in the saddle.'

Sarah Rawl watched helplessly from the parlour window as Caleb Ross escorted his prisoners out of the yard, her emotions of loyalty to family and abhorrence of her brother's actions clashing. As Ross left, the men who had been sent to collect Stretch Crowther's body were riding in with their battered and bloodied load.

In the deepest despair, Sarah Rawl looked at the portrait of her mother over the mantel.

'I guess I'm not real Rawl stock, am I?' she wept bitterly.

*　*　*

By the time the evening shadows were lengthening, and night was creeping over Ghost Creek, Wilfred Lacey had had time to ponder on what his desire to see honest law had led him into. He had suddenly become a leper to be avoided, as the earlier zeal of the citizens to be rid of Dan Bennett and the rottenness he stood for drained away, and their old fears of upsetting Scott Rawl, and particularly his sidekick Jack Sweeney returned to haunt them. The only friend he was left with was the Widow Flannery. She had brought supper to the jail, and had stayed to talk. He had not taken much notice of Kate Flannery up to that time (except to admire her shapely form as every other hot-blooded male in Ghost Creek did), as she did not move in the same social circles as he did.

'I surely appreciate you taking the time to bring me supper, when you're grieving so, ma'am,' he had told her. 'Aren't you afraid like everyone else that Scott Rawl and his cohorts will frown on your actions?'

'If you'll excuse my language, Mr Lacey, I don't give a damn,' she'd said spiritedly. 'I plan on leaving town anyway.'

'That surely would be the town's loss,' he genuinely complimented.

'You bolt that door and stay put once night comes,' she had warned him. 'And how do you intend to stay awake indefinitely?'

'I don't plan to,' Wilfred Lacey said. 'Come first light, I intend to seek out Caleb Ross and pin this badge on him.'

'If you don't mind my saying so, shouldn't you have checked with Mr Ross whether he wanted the marshal's job, instead of assuming that he would?'

Lacey hung his head. 'That would have been the sensible thing to do, ma'am,' he agreed. 'But in my anxiety to see the back of Bennett, I guess I over-reached myself some.'

'Ma'am makes me sound matronly,' the Widow Flannery had said. 'I'd prefer if you called me Kate.'

'That will surely be my pleasure. And you must call me Wilfred, Kate.'

'Now we're both pleasured,' Kate Flannery said, smiling warmly.

In his seven years in Ghost Creek, he had crossed paths with Kate Flannery a thousand times in the bank and in the stores and on the street, but his heart had never before felt such a warm glow as it did then.

'Be sure to keep this door bolted,' she reminded him on leaving.

Being a trained lawyer, he recognized good advice when he heard it.

'I'll be listening for its slide when I leave,' she had told him. 'I'll bring breakfast. Six-thirty OK?'

'I'll look forward to it, Kate.'

He lit the lamp to chase away the shadows, and sat listening to the intense silence. It was as if he was totally alone in Ghost Creek, so eerie was the stillness. It was going to be a long, long night.

★ ★ ★

As the shadows deepened, Caleb Ross fell back aways, leaving enough of a gap between him and his prisoners to give him fair warning of any tricks from Scott Rawl and Jack Sweeney. Whatever he thought about Rawl, who was more wind than brain, and had only recently taken to evil-doing, Sweeney was an entirely different proposition; this would not be his first time heading for jail, Ross figured. And, seeing that he was roaming free, he probably had a bagful of ruses to choose from to avoid the inside of a cell.

Ross had expected the whiff of gunsmoke when he had ridden into the Rawl ranch, and had been taken aback when Rawl and Sweeney decided to go to jail without bullets flying. That was, until he cast his mind back to the *hombre* who wore the star in Ghost Creek, and had understood why Sweeney and Rawl had not made an issue of going to jail. Because, if Ross figured Dan Bennett correctly, they were planning on a token stay in the Ghost Creek poky, and would be back in the saddle as soon as he turned his back.

'Heh, Jack,' Rawl sniggered. 'I reckon that Mr Ross must have ace-good eyesight.' He turned in the saddle. 'Him falling back further all the time.'

Jack Sweeney chuckled. 'Maybe he figures that we'll try and get the drop on him, Scott. Might be fun at that, don't you think?'

'Yeah. It just might at that, Jack,' said Scott Rawl, his tone conveying the pleasure that such an eventuality would give him.

'But we're not like that, Ross,' Sweeney said. 'We're innocent law-abiding citizens. When we get to town, Marshal Bennett will vouch for that.'

Both men laughed uproariously.

Caleb Ross gritted his teeth. Jack Sweeney had just told him what would happen when he delivered them into Bennett's custody.

'You know, fellas,' Ross drawled. 'I figure that, in the interests of fairness, it would be best if I handed you boys over to the law at Danesville.'

Rawl and Sweeney's laughter died a death.

'Danesville!' Scott Rawl barked. 'The marshal at Danesville's got no jurisdiction in these parts.'

'Ain't got no friends either,' Caleb Ross responded smugly. 'Passed through Danesville, on my way here. Talked to the marshal. Seemed a real honest fella. So when I'll explain to him that you've got the Ghost Creek law in your pocket, Rawl, well, I figure that he'll oblige by holding you gents for a US marshal.'

Now it was Jack Sweeney's turn to blanch.

'There ain't no call for a US marshal, Ross,' he growled, suddenly as mean as a stepped-on rattler.

Caleb Ross scratched his stubbled chin.

'Why don't we place the facts before the Danesville lawman, and see if he figures that you fellas have a case to answer?'

'What'll we do, Jack?' Scott Rawl asked, fearfully. 'Tod Clark is the Danesville marshal.'

Jack Sweeney gulped. 'Tod Clark, you say?'

'Seems you know the gent, Mr Sweeney,' Caleb Ross observed, grinning.

'Jack?' Rawl pleaded.

'Shuddup!' Sweeney barked.

'You can't tell me to shut up!' Scott Rawl fumed. 'You work for me.'

'I work for your sister, Rawl,' Sweeney flung back. 'She's the boss of the Rawl ranch.'

'She's a woman,' Rawl scoffed.

Jack Sweeney snorted.

'It might be a kinda funny thing to say,' he said. 'But your sister is more of a man than you'll ever be, you whining windbag.'

Furious, Scott Rawl went to lash out at Sweeney, but the hardcase reacted as fast as a whiplash and swung a pile-driving fist into Rawl's belly, and then leisurely smashed his other fist in Scott Rawl's face. Rawl slumped in his saddle, toppled over and curled up on the ground, retching.

'Are you open to a deal, Ross?' Sweeney asked.

'Maybe,' Ross said. 'What kind of deal have you in mind, Sweeney?'

'I'll give you a written statement, if you can write it, 'cause I can't read or write, saying that Rawl murdered Tom Watson.'

'But that ain't true,' Ross said.

'Well, in a way he did. Watson would never have been in the saloon drowning his sorrows, if Rawl hadn't branded him like a steer. You said as much yourself.'

'I reckon that what you say is true,' Ross said.

'So, with a stretch of imagination, you can see how Rawl is really guilty of Tom Watson's murder, can't ya?'

'You no-good, back-stabbing bastard, Sweeney!' Scott Rawl yelled, between bouts of retching.

For good measure, Jack Sweeney put his boot on Rawl's back and shoved him back into his own vomit.

Caleb Ross could not believe his luck at the rift between the trouble-stirring duo. He decided to play the game a while longer.

'I'll need more, Sweeney,' Ross said.

'More?'

'Well, you and Rawl have been in each other's pockets. So I figure that there's a whole lot more dirt you can dish, Sweeney.'

'Enough to have Rawl breaking rocks for the rest of his life.'

Caleb Ross smiled broadly. 'That sure is sweet music to my ears, Mr Sweeney. So, let's mosey along to Tom Watson's shack. I'm sure Eli Scanell will have a pen or pencil that I can write down what you have to say. Then you can sign it.'

'Then what?'

'Well, I'll have no further use to have you hanging round,' Ross said.

Sweeney's smile was a smug one.

'Let's make fast tracks to the shack,' he said.

'I'll have to ask you to get Rawl back in the saddle,' Ross said.

'Don't you trust me, Ross?' Jack

Sweeney sneered.

'Like I trust a rattler in my pocket,' Caleb Ross replied.

Jack Sweeney laughed snidely. He grabbed Scott Rawl by the scruff of the neck and shoved him on board his horse. Rawl clung precariously to his saddle horn.

'Maybe he'll fall and break his neck,' Sweeney snorted.

'I surely hope not,' Ross said. 'Because, you see, Sweeney, I want a rope round someone's neck for Tom Watson's murder. So,' he swung his horse, 'I suggest that you take real good care of Rawl until we reach the shack and you sign that statement.'

'Lead the way, Ross. I'm in a hurry to shake off the dust of this valley.'

'I'll kill you both!' Scott Rawl ranted, wiping foaming spittle from his mouth, his eyes alive with hatred.

Jack Sweeney slapped his thigh.

'Never knew you were a comedian, Rawl.'

'Sarah was right about you, Sweeney,'

Rawl raged. 'She said you were a toerag, and you are.'

'You know, Scott,' Sweeney said, leaning back in his saddle, 'when my business with Mr Ross is completed, I might just pay your sister a visit before I leave the territory.'

Scott Rawl swallowed hard. The malice in his eyes was replaced by concern.

'You heard him, Ross. Are you going to do nothing?' he pleaded.

Caleb Ross hunched his shoulders.

'After I get Sweeney's signed statement, he's a free man, Rawl.' His tone grew harsh. 'You should have thought of the trouble you were bringing on your sister's shoulders before you got in tow with Sweeney and started trouble in the valley.'

'If I could change things now I surely would, Ross,' Scott Rawl said, remorsefully.

'Well, it's way too late,' Jack Sweeney taunted Rawl.

Eli Scanell came anxiously to the

door of the shack on hearing them approach, the blunderbuss he had held on Ross on their first meeting now primed and ready again.

'It's me, Eli,' Ross called out. 'Caleb Ross.' He feared that in the thickening night, Eli Scanell might have a bad case of jitters.

'You got company, Caleb?' he called out.

'Yeah. I've got company,' Ross called back.

'Who?'

Scanell feared that Ross might be hailing him with a gun prodding his spine.

'Scott Rawl and Jack Sweeney, Eli.'

'Them ain't company,' Eli shouted. 'Them's horse manure, Caleb.'

'You just keep your finger off those triggers,' Caleb Ross said. 'We're coming in, and I'm in charge.'

'Come in facin' the door,' Eli ordered.

The cripple drew back into the darkness of the shack. On hearing the riders approach, he had quenched the lamp. The full moon rising would give light in the clearing in front of the shack. But he would be unseen. He relaxed a little when he saw Caleb Ross ride in freely. And when he dismounted without impediment, Eli relaxed more. However, he still kept a little edginess, just in case.

'Have you got a pencil, Eli?' Ross asked, as he passed inside the shack and relit the lamp.

'Why d'ya want a pencil?' Eli enquired.

'Do you have a darn pencil or nib?' Ross demanded.

'Keep your hair on!' Eli flung back.

He went and rummaged in the drawer of a dresser. He threw the stub of a pencil on to the rough wooden table.

'Do you have writing-paper?' Ross asked.

'What d'ya think this is, a general store?' Eli grumbled.

'Do you?' Ross enquired, exasperated.

'Why d'ya want writin' paper for anyway?'

'Mr Sweeney — '

'Mr?' Eli exclaimed. 'Hah!'

' — is going to give me a statement that Scott Rawl murdered Tom Watson.'

Eli Scanell shuddered in his invalid chair, his face starkly bereft of emotion. Caleb Ross could have kicked his own rear end. Eli did not know that Tom had been killed.

'I told Tom,' Eli said quietly. 'Told him that he'd be killed, if he didn't stop bucking the Rawls.' He looked at Ross. 'Tom Watson was a real gent and a fine man.'

'I know that, Eli,' Ross said gently.

'I'll get that paper now,' Eli said, returning to rummage in the dresser drawer.

★　★　★

Wilfred Lacey was beginning to relax. The night had come alive with the revelry of the saloon. He had often cursed the noise from the watering-hole, when he had been preparing a defence and the rowdy conduct in the saloon set his thoughts awry, but tonight he welcomed the saloon antics. Anything was better than the earlier silence.

I've got me a woman her name is
  Sal.
And she's got a sister who's a real
  pal . . .

The second line of the raucous song was normally full of meaning, but when it was sung by a rogue of an Irishman called Patrick Sean O'Flynn, it had more meaning than it had ever had before.
Lacey chuckled.

And she's got a cousin who likes
  to play
And that's why I'm only half of
  my weight.

Wilfred Lacey's enjoyment of the ribald ditty was interrupted by a noise to the rear of the jail. He went to investigate, but when he arrived in the cells there was nothing to be heard. He was about to return to the office when he heard his name called in a hoarse whisper. He entered the cell from whose barred window he had been summoned, and looked out into the moonlit alley.

'Who's there?' he asked, and got no answer. Angry, he went right up to the window and pressed his face to the bars to get a better view of either side outside of the window. 'I asked who's there?'

Lacey felt a hot sting in his windpipe, and then the awful pain of the stiletto blade as it was twisted. Blood gushed from the hole in his throat. He staggered back, clutching at the blade, knowing that his efforts were futile. His lungs were filling up with the rush of blood. He fell to his knees and then on to his face and lay still, his eyes glazed over in a stare of surprise.

15

Having written down his words, Caleb Ross slid Jack Sweeney's statement across the table for him to sign. Mystified, the hardcase looked at the statement.

'I told ya, Ross. I can't write. Even my name. You sign it for me.'

'Now that wouldn't be legal,' Ross said. 'Tell you what, Sweeney. I'll write down your name on another piece of paper, and then you can copy what I've written on to the paper containing your statement.'

'This sure is taking a lot of time,' Sweeney groused. 'Thought I'd have hit the trail by now, Ross.'

Caleb Ross wrote Jack Sweeney's signature.

'All you've got to do is copy, and we're done,' he said.

Sweeney laboriously copied his signature, and then shoved the statement across the table to Ross. He stood up to leave.

'Got to put a date on that statement to make it legal,' Ross told Sweeney.

'Anythin' you want!' Sweeney snapped. He added the date to his signature.

'Be seein' you folks, I reckon not.' He chuckled. And, turning to Scott Rawl: 'You know, Rawl,' he sneered. 'You're the dumbest critter I've ever milked.'

'I'll find you, Sweeney,' Rawl vowed.

'Well, I ain't scared of ghosts,' the hardcase scoffed. 'And that's what you'll be after they hang you for murder.'

Scott Rawl addressed Caleb Ross:

'Being as you're a friend of Tom Watson, I never figured you'd be as crooked as the likes of Sweeney.'

'I ain't,' Ross said.

On hearing the hammer of a Colt .45 being thumbed back, Jack Sweeney froze in the open doorway. He swung around to face Ross, who was holding the pistol on him.

'Well, not as crooked anyway, Rawl,'

he chuckled. He held up the statement. 'This, Sweeney, is gallows fodder, my friend. You signed a statement all right, but not the statement you figured on.'

Caleb Ross read:

I, Jack Sweeney, do solemnly confess to the murder of Tom Watson at the Golden Ace saloon in the town of Ghost Creek . . .

'You're all wind,' Sweeney snarled. 'Ain't ya?' he asked in desperation a moment later.

Caleb Ross shook his head.

'This is your signed confession, Sweeney. You're as good as hanged.'

'You double-dealing bastard!' Sweeney raged.

'I'll be damned,' Eli Scanell cackled. 'You sure fixed that bastard real good, Caleb.'

'That means I'm off the hook,' Scott Rawl yelled, delightedly.

'Not quite,' Ross said.

'You just said that that statement

hangs Sweeney,' Rawl challenged Ross.

'That it does,' Ross confirmed.

'Then how come — ?'

'You're still going to jail for your cruelty to Tom Watson, Rawl,' said Ross, uncompromisingly.

Jack Sweeney lunged at Ross, a knife appearing in his hand as if by magic. The hardcase proved to be as fast as a mountain cat, and Ross barely avoided the slashing blade. The fury of Sweeney's lunge took him past Ross, who swung round and landed a boot on the hardcase's backside, sending him crashing head first against the far wall of the shack with such momentum that Sweeney's head ruptured the rotten wall and went straight through.

The distraction gave Scott Rawl the chance to wrestle the shotgun from Eli Scanell's grasp. When Caleb Ross turned back from having dealt with Jack Sweeney, he was looking straight down the barrels of the blaster.

'I'm sorry, Caleb,' Eli apologized.

Caleb Ross patted the cripple on the shoulder.

'It's OK, Eli,' he said.

'I ain't going to no jail, Ross,' Scott Rawl declared adamantly, his face flushed and angry, his hands shaking dangerously.

'Easy, Rawl,' Ross cautioned. 'Murder will put a rope round your neck, and that's a whole lot worse than jail.'

'I'm not too sure about that,' Rawl said. 'I couldn't take being locked up, unable to breathe. Heck, I can't sleep in my bedroom with the door closed. There ain't no way that I could survive in a stinking cell.'

By now Jack Sweeney had freed himself from the hole in the shack wall.

'You don't have to go to jail, Scott,' he said. 'We can kill this pair and be across the border before anyone finds their bodies. We can tie rocks to their legs and dump them in the creek.' He laughed. 'It'll be months before anyone will find them — if ever.'

'You expect me to ride with you, after

what you did?' Rawl rasped.

'I wasn't going to leave you behind, Scott,' Sweeney purred. 'We're partners, ain't we? Now what kind of a man do you think I am? Shucks, Scott, I'd never run out on a partner.'

A look of confusion spread across Scott Rawl's face.

'I was going to wait outside 'til you came out with Ross,' Jack Sweeney crooned. 'Then I was going to ambush him and set you free.'

Sweeney was a very skilful liar. And, panicked and bewildered, Scott Rawl was easy prey to Sweeney's temptation and persuasion.

'If you listen to him, Rawl,' Caleb Ross said. 'You're even a bigger fool than I thought you were.'

'Don't listen to him, Scott,' Sweeney coaxed. 'If you do, you'll be breaking rocks for the rest of your natural. How do you figure that branding a man with a branding-iron, just like you would a steer, will sound in court? Goddam awful, that's how it'll sound, Scott!'

Sweeney went on: 'Pull that trigger, Scott. Kill Ross. The cripple ain't a problem. I'll cut his throat and enjoy doing it, too.'

'Don't be a fool, Rawl,' Caleb Ross advised. 'The law will hunt you down, for sure.'

'The law can only catch us if they know where we are, Ross,' Sweeney said. 'We'll be old men by the time anyone finds these critters, once I've done with them, Scott.'

Jack Sweeney ran a finger round inside his collar, and drew in deep breaths.

'Darn, it's kinda hard to breathe in here, ain't it folks?'

Immediately, Scott Rawl began to gasp for breath. Sweeney stepped back a pace and sneered at Ross. He had cleverly played on Scott Rawl's fear of confined spaces, and as Ross watched the terror taking Rawl over, he knew that his and Eli Scanell's lives hung by a thread.

'Close your ears to Sweeney, Rawl,'

Ross urged the panicked rancher.

'Imagine, Scott,' Sweeney whispered breathlessly, 'Stinking air that you can't breathe. That's what prison means.' Scott Rawl began to heave for breath. 'Blast Ross, Scott,' the hardcase purred. 'It's the only way you're going to stay out of jail.'

Scott Rawl was nodding in agreement. Sweat poured from his facial pores. His raw scent of fear filled the shack. Ross braced himself. Any second now he'd be ripped apart by the fury of the shotgun.

16

Scott Rawl's eyes glowed crazily. His shoulders heaved with the effort of breathing. His finger pressed on the trigger of the Greener. Caleb Ross's gaze was riveted on the barrels of the shotgun, from where, any second now, certain death would be delivered.

'Don't do it, boy,' Eli Scanell pleaded. 'Even if you're never caught, there's no way back for a man to peace of mind from cold-blooded murder.'

'I ain't a boy, cripple!' Scott Rawl bellowed.

Then, suddenly, to Caleb Ross's utter astonishment, Scott Rawl calmed. His breathing became easier, and the glow of craziness in his eyes faded.

'Do it!' Jack Sweeney roared, on seeing sense replacing madness in Scott Rawl. 'Give me the damn gun and I'll do it for ya!'

'No,' Rawl said calmly. 'I'm no murderer, Sweeney, and I want no part of murder either. I've been a fool.' He turned to face Caleb Ross. 'What I did to Tom Watson, was the lowest thing a man could do to another man, even one he considered his enemy. I can only say that for some time past the devil's been in me.'

'A man can change. And you've made a good start, Rawl,' Ross said.

'Some day, when I get the courage, I'll ride back this way and take the punishment due to me for my cruelty to Watson. But until I get that courage, I guess the only thing I can do is hit the trail with Sweeney.'

'Now you're talking sense,' Jack Sweeny said. 'Let's ride.'

'That's a mistake added to mistakes, Rawl,' Caleb Ross opined. 'Best to face your punishment and your demons right now. That way, with the slate wiped clean, you can live a contented life here in the valley. Otherwise, you'll spend your days looking over your shoulder, because riding with a no-good like Sweeney will bring continual trouble.'

'I don't plan to be in his company for long, Ross,' Rawl said.

'The minute it will take to walk out that door and ride away will be too long to be in Sweeney's company,' Ross said.

'I don't see any other way out of this right now,' Scott Rawl said, with finality. 'I'd be obliged if you'd explain to Sarah, and tell her that I'm sorry. Tell her also that she can trust Ben Haggerty to ramrod the ranch for her. He'll fire those needing firing, and put to rights the neglect I've been guilty of.'

'I'll tell your sister what you said,' Caleb Ross promised the downhearted rancher.

'Come on.'

Jack Sweeney dragged Scott Rawl with him. Rawl shrugged him off.

'Tell sis that she's an ace, Ross.'

'I'll tell her.'

'I'll be damned,' Eli Scanell said in awe when they had left. 'Never thought

I'd see Scott Rawl repentant.'

Caleb Ross hurried to the door to watch Rawl and Sweeney gallop off, and to confirm his worst fears. They had taken his horse in tow, leaving him helplessly stranded.

★ ★ ★

Murder done, Dan Bennett slipped from the alley alongside the jail. Finding Main empty, he hurried along to the end of the street to the clapboard house that went with the marshal's job, to collect his saddle bags, stuffed with the loot that his association with Scott Rawl had put his way. He had taken his revenge on Wilfred Lacey, and he'd be long gone before anyone found the lawyer's body.

However, the street was not entirely empty. And if Bennett had glanced into the shadows of the general store's recessed doorway, he'd have seen a witness to his feverish escape from the scene of his crime.

'Where the hell can I get a horse fast, Eli?' Caleb Ross demanded.

'The nearest would be Jake Barrington's ranch, Caleb.'

'You don't sound very hopeful, Eli,' Ross said.

'That's 'cause I ain't. By the time you'd reach the Barrington ranch on foot, Scott Rawl and Jack Sweeney would have died in Mexico of old age.'

Caleb Ross slammed his fist against the wall of the shack, punching another hole in its rotten timber.

'Darn,' Eli Scanell whined. 'There'll be more holes in the shack than wall!'

★ ★ ★

Kate Flannery, on her way to check on Wilfred Lacey's well-being, was curious when she observed Dan Bennett slide out of the alley alongside the jail like a viper about to strike, and she stepped back into the shadows of the general

196

store's door. As he passed her hiding-place, he chuckled evilly. When it was safe to do so, she continued on to the law office, a deep apprehension hurrying her steps.

*　*　*

Caleb Ross was pacing the shack floor, trying desperately to find a way round his problem, when Scott Rawl staggered through the doorway and collapsed, blood streaming from a head wound.

'Sweeney hit me with a rock,' he mumbled.

'Did you arrive on your nag?' Ross enquired urgently.

Scott Rawl nodded, then passed out.

Ross examined the gash on Scott Rawl's head and saw that, though it was an ugly, ragged wound, it had not done any damage that was not repairable. He picked Rawl up and laid him on the bed.

'Can you clean his wound up, Eli?' he asked.

'Sure I can.' Ross was at the door when he asked: 'Where're you headed?'

'To the Rawl ranch,' Ross replied brusquely. 'That's where I figure Jack Sweeney will head for. Besides lusting for Sarah Rawl, there'll also be cash in the safe for the day-to-day running of the ranch.'

★   ★   ★

'Wilfred,' Kate Flannery called for the second time, slapping on the law office door with the flat of her hand, her apprehension turning to outright fear as she instinctively knew that Dan Bennett had done Lacey a mischief. She tugged and pulled at the bolted door, to no avail.

'Somethin' wrong, Kate?' a tipsy man passing by on his way home from the saloon enquired.

'I think something's happened to Mr Lacey, Ned,' she said.

'Let me try,' Ned said, and charged the door. The door bounced him back on his backside. 'Wait right here, Kate,' he said, nursing his bruises.

The man called Ned ran across the street to the saloon and reappeared in seconds with the brawny town blacksmith in tow. Ed Benning was a giant with the poundage to match. The door of the marshal's office was no obstacle for him, and it shattered on his first charge. Kate Flannery ran inside. Wilfred Lacey was nowhere to be seen, but the door leading to the cells was open. She hurried to the cells, and came up short on seeing Wilfred Lacey lying in a pool of his own blood.

'Who'd do this?' Ed Benning wanted to know, horrified on seeing the blood-encrusted stiletto protruding from Lacey's windpipe.

'I know who,' Kate Flannery said, with a quiet fury. 'But knowing won't bring Wilfred back.'

On hearing the catch in her voice, Ned and Ed Benning exhanged curious looks. Although she had been in Ghost Creek for several years, that night was the first time she had spoken to the town lawyer. Western towns had strict social codes, and they had moved in different circles. Alec Flannery had been a decent, hard-working man when sober but that had not qualified him to be part of Ghost Creek's social élite. She had found Wilfred Lacey to be a courteous and warm-hearted man with whom, when the hurt of losing Tom Watson mellowed with time, she could have been friends — good friends, too, she'd reckoned.

★   ★   ★

Jack Sweeney was lurking outside the den window, lustfully watching Sarah Rawl sitting by a log-fire, lost in her thoughts and looking mightily depressed. His heart beat like a war drum, and his mouth was sand-dry. The intensity of the fire in his groin left him breathless.

The first day he had ridden into the Rawl ranch his only concern had been to bum a meal and if possible a bed for the night. Ranching was hard work, and he had never had an affinity with bending his back in labour. His was a life of saloons and bawdy-houses, and he'd much prefer to swindle for a living than work for it. He had thought that if he were shown hospitality, he could maybe deal poker in the bunkhouse from a very special deck that had six aces, and then, an hour before cock-crow, he had planned to help himself to anything that would turn a dollar for him. The last ranch house in which he had been shown hospitality found that the next morning every item of silver had vanished. They had also found a maid very distressed, gagged and tied to the bed, and half-insane from the way he had used her.

That was the plan until he saw Sarah Rawl. And from that second on, he had lusted after her. Now the time to have her had come, and he hoped that his heart would not give out first, so furiously was it beating.

He was in luck, Sarah Rawl was beginning to doze.

He checked the yard and its environs for any sign of life and saw none. The bunkhouse was quiet and still, with no light showing.

Sarah Rawl's head bowed lower, and she began to breathe in long, even breaths. Jack Sweeney slipped the catch of the window with his knife with the deftness of long practice. Slowly and carefully, he slid the lower half of the window up and stepped through into the den. Sarah Rawl slept on. He closed the window as carefully and as patiently as he had opened it and stood stock-still, watching the woman he had desired for so long. Smiling, his gaze went to the open wall safe behind her. He was pleased that he would not have to waste time persuading her to open the safe; time he'd now have to pleasure himself all the more.

★　★　★

Caleb Ross pushed Rawl's mare to her limit, unheeding, in his hurry to reach the Rawl ranch, of the night-enshrouded terrain. Sweeney had a sizeable head start on him. Luckily for Ross, the mare knew the terrain. At full gallop, Ross prayed that he'd be on time to save Sarah Rawl from Jack Sweeney's vileness.

As he rode, a terrible anger built up inside him: an anger that Caleb Ross came to understand. Sarah Rawl had made by far a greater impression on him than he had been willing to admit up to now.

★　★　★

Bulging saddle-bags having been retrieved from under the floorboards, Dan Bennett gleefully readied himself to quit Ghost Creek. He mounted up and rode stealthily along the main street. There was really no danger to a safe passage; the saloon had closed and the town had settled down for the night. Therefore, his surprise was total when, from opposite alleys, men came to block his progress.

'Going somewhere, Bennett,' the owner of the general store rasped.

Bennett turned his horse to go the other way, ready now to leave town at a gallop. But men had also gathered behind him to cut off his retreat.

'What's going on?' Bennett blustered.

Ed Benning, the blacksmith, stepped forward, a massive block of a man.

'What were you doing behind the jail tonight, Bennett?' he quizzed.

'Behind the jail?' Bennett hedged. 'What kind of crazy question is that, Benning?'

'Do you deny that you were behind the jail, then?' the general storekeeper questioned.

'I ain't been outside the house all night,' Bennett declared.

'You're a liar, Bennett!'

Dan Bennett peered into the darkness of the boardwalk to find his accuser. Kate Flannery showed herself from the recessed doorway of the general store. 'I saw you come out of the alley near the jail, after you murdered Wilfred Lacey. I was hiding right here in this doorway.'

'You're loco!' Bennett growled.

'We don't think so,' Ed Benning said, waving a mallet of a hand to include the men with him. 'We reckon that Kate's got it right, Bennett.'

'I ain't standing for any more of this,' Bennett said, and walked his horse forward. But the crowd blocked his passage.

'Those are mighty fat saddle-bags you've got there,' the town blacksmith observed. 'I think we should take a look inside.'

'None of your damn business, Benning!' Bennett barked.

'I figure its the loot he's earned doing Scott Rawl's dirty work for him,' an angry man in the crowd shouted. 'Like backing up Jack Sweeney's mossy yarn when he murdered Tom Watson in cold blood.'

There was angry agreement from the crowds in front and behind Bennett as they closed in threateningly. Bennett blanched. He'd seen what angry crowds could do. In fact he had led many of those angry mobs for fun and reward.

'This town is placing you under arrest for the murder of Wilfred Lacey, Bennett,' the owner of the general store and the town council's deputy chairman said.

The former marshal of Ghost Creek drew his sixgun and blasted over the heads of his impeders. 'Move,' he ordered. 'Or I'll start laying lead into you.'

Slowly, the crowd ahead of him parted.

'Sensible,' Bennett snorted.

He cockily rode through the path that had opened up for him, threatening each side with his sixgun. A rifle cracked. The cocky grin on Dan Bennett's face froze. A flash of surprise lit his eyes, before he tumbled from his horse. No one asked who had shot him, because no one in Ghost Creek cared or wanted to know.

Ed Benning opened the saddle-bags. They were bursting with bundles of dollar bills.

'I think this will just about build that new school we've been talking about,' he said, holding the saddle-bags aloft.

★　★　★

Sarah Rawl's eyes opened sleepily, and took a while to focus and make sense of the shadow leaning over her. When she did make sense of it, and Jack Sweeney's bloated and sweating face leapt into view, he quickly smothered her attempted scream.

'Now you be a good girl.' He leered. 'But not too good, mind.' His features hardened. 'Try to scream again and I'll slit your damn throat, woman.'

Sarah fought him tooth and nail, but she was no match for the hardcase. He slapped her hard across the face, bringing a stream of blood from her nose. His hands clawed at her blouse.

'No,' Sarah pleaded. 'Please, no.'

Jack Sweeney's lust-contorted face held no sympathy or mercy.

'You'll enjoy it, Miss Rawl.' He chuckled, unbuckling his gunbelt and then the belt of his trousers.

As Caleb Ross crashed through the den window, Jack Sweeney's trousers dropped and hindered him as he turned round to face Ross. The hardcase was an easy target for a series of swift and punishing blows that ended in Sweeney sliding down the den wall, unconscious.

Sarah Rawl fled to the comfort of Caleb Ross's arms. He soothed away her sobbing. Preoccupied as he was, he did not see Sweeney crawl along the floor to the desk where he knew he'd find a sixgun in the drawer. With just a breath to spare, Ross shoved Sarah Rawl aside. His pistol flashed from leather and blasted. The gunblast pitched Jack Sweeney back against the wall, but this time he would not be getting up.

'That's it, neighbour,' Scott Rawl said to Caleb Ross, who had held the last post of the boundary fence separating the smaller Fat Belly ranch from the sprawling Rawl range, for him to hammer home. Rawl held out a hand. 'Welcome to the valley, Caleb.'

Caleb Ross took Scott Rawl's hand and shook it heartily and warmly.

'Thanks for giving me the chance to amount to something, Caleb,' Scott Rawl said.

Caleb Ross had thought long and hard about what a fitting punishment for Scott Rawl's cruelty to Tom Watson should be. But in the end, he had decided that charity and forgiveness would reap a better harvest than punishment. And, a year on, on seeing the Rawl range back to its former glory and neighbourly relations the order of the day in the valley, he took pride in that decision. And he figured that Tom Watson would have, too.

'Saw Sarah in town, leading a band of ruffians across the street from the school to the church, looking mighty pleased and perky,' Ross said.

Scott Rawl laughed heartily.

'Sis couldn't wait to be rid of cows and grass, and get back to teaching.' Rawl considered Ross. 'I'd be pleased if you came to the house for dinner on Sunday, Caleb. Kate Flannery has settled in real well as housekeeper.' He rubbed his expanding gut. 'Too well, maybe. Be hard to see her leave,' he said thoughtfully. 'That's if she ever decides to.'

'A woman like Kate needs roots, Scott,' Caleb Ross said. Scott Rawl nodded his head in agreement. 'I reckon, given the chance, she'd live out her days in the valley.'

'You figure,' Scott said, rubbing his chin.

'I figure,' Ross assured him.

Scott Rawl grinned. 'Sarah will be along Sunday.'

Scott Rawl swung into the saddle and

rode off across the lush range, scattering protesting cows.

'Seems to me that all the hard work putting up that boundary line was wasted,' Eli Scanell said.

'How do you figure that, Eli?' Ross asked.

'Well, it'll be coming down again, that's what I figure.'

'Coming down!' Ross yelped.

'Soon, too, I reckon. When you and Sarah Rawl stop pretendin' you ain't keen on each other, and tie the knot. Then there'll be no need for darn fences.'

'You know, Eli Scanell,' Ross grunted, 'sometimes you talk real horse manure!'

'If you don't believe old Eli, kiss her on Sunday and see if she kisses you back.'

Caleb Ross laughed.

'You know, Eli,' he said, 'maybe I'll do just that.'

'I know damn well you will.' Eli Scanell cackled.

We do hope that you have enjoyed reading this large print book.

Did you know that all of our titles are available for purchase?

We publish a wide range of high quality large print books including:
Romances, Mysteries, Classics
General Fiction
Non Fiction and Westerns

Special interest titles available in large print are:
The Little Oxford Dictionary
Music Book, Song Book
Hymn Book, Service Book

Also available from us courtesy of Oxford University Press:
Young Readers' Dictionary
(large print edition)
Young Readers' Thesaurus
(large print edition)

For further information or a free brochure, please contact us at:
Ulverscroft Large Print Books Ltd.,
The Green, Bradgate Road, Anstey,
Leicester, LE7 7FU, England.
Tel: (00 44) **0116 236 4325**
Fax: (00 44) **0116 234 0205**

MARSHAL LAW

Corba Sunman

Deputy Marshal Jed Law was sent to Buffalo Crossing to keep the peace; a bloody feud between two ranchers had already cost a man his life. But Law's real troubles started when he first set eyes on Julie Rutherford and her father Ben . . . Opposed by hard cases determined to wipe him out, he would be forced to shoot his way through. And worse was to come . . . Law would need his pistol loaded and ready to use until the last desperate shot.

HOT LEAD RANGE

Jack Holt

When an undercover agent going by the name of Bob Harker arrives in Sweetwater Valley, his task is to prevent a range war developing: the ruthless Butch Collins intends to claim the entire valley by forcing out his neighbours. One such neighbour is Frank Bateman — Harker's old boss when he was a Pinkerton detective. Harker manages to infiltrate the Collins outfit but, forced to take ever greater risks, could this be his final mission?

BADLANDERS

Ben Nicholas

The mining town of Sundown was running into chaos. When the sheriff faltered and shots sounded, hard-case miners took to the streets — fired up and ready for a showdown with anyone who stood in their way. Shane Carson was waiting for them at the jailhouse. Carson was no lawman, but he was a man on a mission — even if that meant standing alone against a murderous rabble. But could anybody hope to stand against such odds and live?

THE JAYHAWKERS

Elliot Conway

Luther Kane, one-time captain with Colonel Mosby's raiders, is forced to leave Texas; bounty hunters are tracking down and arresting men who served with the colonel during the Civil War. He joins up with three Missouri brush boys, outlawed by the Union government, and themselves hunted for atrocities committed whilst riding with 'Bloody' Bill Anderson. Now, in a series of bloody shoot-outs, they must take the fight to the red-legs to finally end the war against them . . .

VENGEANCE AT BITTERSWEET

Dale Graham

Always a loner, Largo reckoned it was the reason for his survival as a bounty hunter. But things change when he has to join forces with Colonel Sebastian Kyte in the hunt for a band of desperate killers. Kyte is not interested in financial rewards. So what is the old Confederate soldier's game? And how does a Kiowa medicine man's daughter figure in the final showdown at Bittersweet? Vengeance is sweet, but it comes with a heavy price tag.